W9-BEB-274

A BLAST FROM THE PAST

"Do you know what that is?"

"An airplane," Sheryl answered simply.

"It's a Mustang—a P Fifty-one! It's a World War Two bomber escort," Rick said as he watched the Mustang follow the Visitor craft through a series of rolls. He told himself it was impossible. Dogfights like this didn't happen anymore, except in war movies.

"He's got 'em!" Sheryl Lee's arms went around Rick's neck, hugging him in unabandoned joy. "He's got 'em!"

A plume of greasy black smoke erupted from the tail of the skyfighter. Abruptly, the Visitor ship dipped, diving toward the ground. It did not pull up from this maneuver but plowed into the earth.

Overhead the Mustang did a victory roll, banked eastward, and disappeared over the horizon.

Other V books from Pinnacle

V

THE TEXAS RUN

Geo. W. Proctor

PINNACLE BOOKS   NEW YORK

ATTENTION: SCHOOLS AND CORPORATIONS

PINNACLE Books are available at quantity discounts with
bulk purchases for educational, business or special promo-
tional use. For further details, please write to: SPECIAL
SALES MANAGER, Pinnacle Books, Inc., 1430
Broadway, New York, NY 10018.

This novel is a work of fiction. Names, characters, places, and
incidents are either the product of the author's imagination or are
used fictitiously. Any resemblance to actual events or places or
persons, living or dead, is entirely coincidental.

V: THE TEXAS RUN

Copyright © 1985 by Warner Bros., Inc.

All rights reserved, including the right to reproduce this book or
portions thereof in any form.

An original Pinnacle Books edition, published for the first time
anywhere.

First printing/September 1985

ISBN: 0-523-42470-1
Can. ISBN: 0-523-43444-8

Printed in the United States of America

PINNACLE BOOKS, INC.
1430 Broadway
New York, New York 10018

9   8   7   6   5   4   3   2   1

For Lana—thank you for being.

THE TEXAS RUN

Chapter 1

A shadow moved within the shadows. At the periphery of Rick Hurley's vision a patch of gray like a watery, blurred human form darted from the light.

Rick snapped around. The muzzle of his Uzi leaped up, sweeping from left to right, ready to meet an attack.

"What is it, Rick?" Michael Donovan's head jerked to the left. The former news cameraman's eyes narrowed as he stared at his young companion. Questioning creases furrowed his high brow.

"Thought I saw something move over there." Rick tilted his head toward the muted glow of hangar lights fifty yards to the south.

Twenty pairs of eyes probed the fog blanketing John Wayne International Airport. Twenty heads cocked from side to side, listening to the night.

"Nothing," Donovan whispered. "There's nothing out there, Rick, except fog."

"Yeah." Rick Hurley eased aside a strand of blond hair plastered against his forehead by sweat and mist. "Must be imagining things."

"It's the night." Donovan reassuringly squeezed Rick's shoulder and smiled in sympathy. "The fog's getting to all of us."

Rick nodded in acceptance, although his right forefinger remained curled around the trigger of his machine pistol.

The resistance leader's gaze and those of the men and

women in his command returned to the barely discernible form of a Visitor squad vehicle squatted on the runway ahead of them. Bathed by mist-diffused airport lights, the alien craft's white form appeared to glow like some phantasmic wingless insect. Beside a gaping door midway along the ship's angular segmented body stood two red-uniformed demons—shock troopers with energy rifles clutched across their chests.

Rick's attention returned to the line of hangars to the left. His blue-gray eyes probed the dense fog that rolled off the Pacific Ocean to accompany the first cool breath of autumn. The hangars' lights revealed only mist swirling and shifting in a gentle night breeze.

The twenty-two-year-old resistance fighter silently cursed. He was *certain* that he had seen someone or some*thing* step from the darkness separating the second and third hangars, then dart back into the cloaking blackness. Now there was nothing.

"Relax, Rick," Mike Donovan whispered. "We've got the jump on the lizards this time. There's no way for them to suspect anything."

"Yeah, I know." Rick managed a weak, unconvincing smile for the Los Angeles resistance leader. "Like you said, it's the fog getting to me. I'm all right."

"Good, because I want you to position your group among those hangars as soon as we're through the fence," Donovan answered.

"Can do." Rick's gaze darted back to the hangars half hidden in the fog—nothing. "Just get us through the fence, give us five minutes, and we'll be ready."

Donovan nodded and turned to his right. "Ed, Norton, cut the fence."

Two men separated from their companions and crawled on their bellies from the drainage ditch that concealed the resistance assault team. Their movement a soft whisper in the mist-drenched grass, they edged to the eight-foot-high chain-link fence encircling the Orange

County airport. A dull snap touched Rick's ears when the wire cutters bit through the first link in the mesh barrier.

Rick's gaze surveyed the airport once again. Except for the Visitor squad vehicle and its two human-disguised reptilian guards, it was deserted, as were all Los Angeles area airports each night. The nightly closing of airports, even John Wayne International, was but one of the numerous concessions the provisional government had made to the invaders from Sirius' fourth planet so that Los Angeles might retain its status as a modern-day Lisbon in a world fighting tooth and claw for its very life.

Shut down the airports and it's easier to keep the human cattle in their pens each night, he thought bitterly.

The aliens needed Earth for its vast water supply, having polluted the meager waters of their own world. As for the inhabitants of the planet they sought to conquer, cattle was exactly what human beings were to the Visitors. The carnivorous reptiles viewed every man, woman, and child as beef on the hoof, animals to be bred, butchered, and devoured.

And the quislings of the provisional government are playing right into the Visitors' hands! Hate and anger welled in Rick's breast.

The Los Angeles resistance had led the fight to drive the Visitors from Earth and had developed the red toxin that eventually sent the aliens fleeing back into the yawning void of space. When the second alien assault came, aided by the fact that the poisonous bacteria was ineffectual in Earth's tropical and subtropical zones, Los Angeles, rather than mounting an offensive against the unearthly invaders, had formed a provisional government to serve as a liaison between the aliens and the world's human authorities.

At the chain-link fence Ed lifted an arm and waved his companions forward.

"Okay, let's move out," Mike Donovan said. "All of

you know what to do. Keep low and quiet until the snakes arrive with their pigeon."

Without another word Donovan pushed from the ditch and crawled toward the gaping rent Ed and Norton held open in the fence. Right behind the former television cameraman, Rick Hurley moved through the fence and waited for the four men and women in his group to gather at his side.

Still belly down in the soaked grass, Rick maneuvered his command behind a line of trash containers. A quick check assured him their movements went unnoticed. However, a hundred feet of wide-open and unprotected space separated them from the side of the first hangar. He rose in a crouch and turned to his companions.

"We cross one at a time," he said. "I go first. Marion follows me, then Gus and Edith. Jim, you have to protect our backsides as well as your own."

James Leard, a senior member of a Los Angeles civil law firm before the Visitors' invasion, nodded, accepting his role as rear guard. Rick returned the nod, double-checked the Uzi's safety, making certain it was off and that the machine pistol was set to automatic, then darted from the shadows of the trash containers.

He ran without a glance to the runway and the Visitor shock troopers who stood guard there. With each long stride he expected to hear the high-pitched whine of an energy burst come in counterpoint to his wildly beating heart. The aliens' weapons still remained silent when he reached the hangar's veiling shadow.

Back pressed against the cool surface of the structure's wall, Rick drew a steadying breath before cautiously poking his head around the side of the building. The pair of shock troopers stood like statues beside the squad vehicle.

Lifting a hand, he signaled Marion from behind the trash containers. Like a sprinter breaking out of starting blocks, the black-haired woman dashed toward his position. Seconds later she was at his side, breath coming quick and shallow. He waved Gus to him.

While the forty-five-year-old janitor ran toward the hangar, Rick felt a familiar sensation suffuse his chest, one he had experienced on every resistance mission in which he had participated. Without shame, he gave a name to that warm sensation—pride!

These men and women were not warriors drilled into a crack fighting unit by the military. They were simply people one would expect to find living next door, if the world had not been turned upside down by the Visitors. Everyday women and men who willingly placed their lives on the line day and night for that intangible thing human beings called freedom.

To Rick any of the twenty who had followed Mike Donovan to John Wayne was worth more than the whole damned Los Angeles provisional government. Yet it was for a member of that cowardly group of bureaucrats that those here tonight risked their lives.

Gus ducked into the shadows. Rick waved Edith after him, trying not to think about the goal of tonight's mission. Their reason for being here would not leave his head.

Three hours ago the resistance's intelligence network had intercepted a Visitor communiqué. That message outlined plans to abduct a member of the provisional government, bring him to John Wayne International, and secrete him aboard the Visitor Mother Ship that floated above Los Angeles. There, within the aliens' conversion chamber, the Visitors' Scientific Commander Diana would remold his brain until he was no more than a walking zombie willing to perform any task asked of him.

Rick grunted with disgust as he signaled James to the hangar. Saving a turncoat from a lizard brainwashing wasn't the young man's idea. However, Mike Donovan had explained that if they could break up tonight's activities, the Visitors would be beaten on another front. Plus, there was always the chance of winning the governmental muckety-muck over to their side. And it never hurt to have friends in high places.

"They still look like statues out on the runway," James said when he joined his companions. "They haven't moved except to circle the squad vehicle now and then."

"So far so good." Rick glanced at his wristwatch. A minute remained of the five within which he had promised Donovan to have his group positioned. "Move out."

Reaching the back side of the wall, Rick glanced behind the hangars. Only darkness and night greeted him. Edging around the corner of the building, he stepped toward the second hangar, pausing only to assure himself no Visitors lay hidden between the structures before hastening toward the third of the massive buildings.

He approached the opening between the second and third hangars with greater caution. Ready to jerk back immediately, he looked down the alleylike space between the two buildings. An overheld breath softly escaped his lips. The passage between the hangars was empty except for two garbage cans.

He shook his head. This was the very spot that he had thought he had seen movement earlier. *Maybe my eyes were playing tricks on me*.

"Gus, Edith, in here and keep low." Rick motioned the man and woman between the hangars.

He and his two remaining companions stepped onto the area between the third and fourth hangars. Again no waiting snakes in human disguise were discovered. The trio worked through the shadows toward the glow coming from the front of the structures. Three feet from the front of the hangars, Rick halted his friends and inched forward.

The squad vehicle with its two Visitor guards sat directly between their position and the airport's terminal. He tried to locate the rest of the resistance team, but saw nothing. All else was fog and night. That was good. The last thing they needed was to be sighted before the Visitors arrived with their prisoner.

Rick looked back at Marion and James. "Now we make ourselves comfortable and wait."

The three squatted on their heels, eyes focused on the squad vehicle.

For the thousandth time in the past five minutes, Rick stared at the face of his watch. *Two o'clock.* At least two lifetimes had passed while the minute hand made one complete circuit. The blond resistance fighter bit dubiously at his lower lip.

"Maybe the snakes changed airports on us?" James' question echoed Rick's own unspoken thought.

"Or maybe they got wind that we were onto them," Rick suggested with a shrug.

"Want me to find Mike and see if he knows what's going—"

"Lights!" Marion interrupted, pointing across the runway. "There—to the left of the terminal."

Rick saw them now. A single pair of automobile headlights glowed like dull luminous eyes in the mist. The spots of light vanished when the car wheeled around the terminal. Then they were back, growing larger and brighter as they moved directly for the Visitor craft.

"This is it." Rick stood, checking the 9mm machine pistol one last time. He patted the pockets of his blue jeans and jacket, pleased by the solid weight of ten additional twenty-round clips of Teflon personal-armor-piercing bullets. "As soon as the car stops by the squad vehicle, go for it."

The distinctive form of a Lincoln Continental slid beneath the airport's lights. The sedan's sleek body style, complete with decorative exhaust slots located on each side just behind the front wheels, and its silver-gray body aglisten with the mist's moisture all gave the vehicle the appearance of a blunt-nosed shark slicing through the fog. The image evoked an involuntary shiver that worked up Rick's spine when the car slowed and stopped beside the squad vehicle.

"Let's go!" Rick raised the compact Israeli-made Uzi and ran into the light with his four companions right behind him.

Abandoning their hiding places, the remaining fifteen members of the resistance force pushed through the fog, surrounding the Visitor craft in a circle. The ship's two guards came to life. In confusion they jerked from one side to another as though uncertain how to meet the advancing ring of human fighters.

"Throw down your weapons!" Mike Donovan's voice rang out, echoing across the deserted airport. "All we want is the man you're holding in the car."

The muzzles of the guards' energy rifles dipped. Hesitantly, the aliens' fingers unwrapped from the weapons. The blue-black rifles fell to the tarmac with ringing metallic clanks.

Tension tautened every muscle of Rick's body. Doubt gnawed at his mind. What was going on? Snakes didn't surrender! Still the resistance's circle tightened.

In the next moment the answer to Rick's question became all too obvious.

Simultaneously, beams of glaring white light from the bellies of two squad vehicles hidden in the dense fog overhead bathed the runway from above, the doors to the sedan swung open, and six red-uniformed shock troopers leaped from the vehicle. A split second later a line of Visitor soldiers piled from the interior of the squad vehicle on the ground.

Chaos reigned!

The instant it took Rick's mind to accept what his eyes

saw and comprehend the trap they had blindly walked into, the shock troopers opened fire. Sizzling beams of blue-white energy seared the night.

A woman screamed.

From the corner of his eye, Rick saw an actinic burst slice into the chest of Lea Beeman. Flames flared on the blue Dodgers' baseball jacket the young woman wore as she crumpled and collapsed to the runway.

A piteous cry of horror and pain tore from the young man's throat. Lea had been a fellow student at UCLA and had recruited him into the resistance.

Rick reacted rather than thought. His finger tightened around the Uzi's trigger and squeezed. Yellow and blue flames burst from the machine pistol's muzzle. A deadly accurate spray of twenty 9mm slugs spat at knee level cut into the small army of shock troopers charging from the alien craft.

"Back!" Rick shouted to the men and women under his command while he jerked a fresh clip from a back pocket and slammed it into the Uzi. "Get the hell out of here!"

Neither of the four protested. Squeezing off short bursts of cover fire from their own weapons, they retreated into the protective shadows of the hangars.

The staccato barking of machine pistols drowned the hissing whine of energy weapons when Rick's eyes lifted to the mass of Visitor warriors again. Teflon-coated bullets ripped through the black flak-jacket-like personal armor the shock troopers wore over their chests. They fell, unearthly reptilian death cries yowling from throats born on a world more than eight light-years from the planet they sought to conquer.

A humorless smile lifted the corners of Rick's mouth when he unleashed another twenty-round burst into Visitor soldiers. The trap the aliens sought to spring had a bottleneck—the door on the side of the squad vehicle.

The shock troopers couldn't get through it quickly enough to disperse and attack effectively.

Ejecting the empty clip, Rick pulled another from his jeans and slipped it into the machine pistol. While he backstepped toward the hangars, he turned his attention to the overhead lights, which transformed night into day.

The two additional Visitor squad vehicles still hovered twenty-five feet above the runway. Searchlights glared from their undersides, illuminating the battle below. Rick lifted the Uzi, sighted on the nearest of the shuttles, and opened fire.

Glass shattered, and for an instant fire flared. Then night returned—or at least a portion of the darkness. The second Visitor ship still spilled a flood of light over the scene beneath it.

Intent on blinding the remaining squad vehicle, Rick once more ejected his gun's empty clip and dug into a jacket pocket for another twenty rounds. A whining blast of heat and light tore into the tarmac at his feet. All thought of shooting out searchlights was fogotten.

Five shock troopers broke from their companions and charged him with rifles spitting streams of pulse-beam energy. Unwilling to risk the possibility that the shock troopers' armor might deflect his bullets, Rick once again aimed at knee level and squeezed the Uzi's trigger. In this case, an immobile lizard, legs shot out from under him, was just as good as a dead one.

Three of the shock troopers dropped, sprawling facedown on the runway with rifles careening from their hands. A fourth staggered, then fell clutching his left knee. The fifth, however, kept coming, his energy rifle spraying bursts of deadly blue-white beams into the night.

With the machine pistol empty and no time to load another clip to meet the attack, Rick took the only option open to him. He turned and ran, zigzagging toward the protection of the hangars. At the same time he managed to empty the spent clip, extract another from his jacket, and slip it into the Uzi.

Reaching the opening between two of the massive structures, he darted into the veiling shadows, turned, fired a short burst at his pursuer, then continued his flight. The effort was wasted energy. Beams from the Visitor's rifle sizzled down the corridor between the hangars, seeking an elusive target that dodged back and forth between the walls.

The weaving race was little more than a waltz with death, and Rick knew it. What he had hoped would be protection had turned into a murderous alley with no apparent escape. It was only a matter of time until the random bursts the shock trooper fired down the passage struck home. Accidentally or not, the results would be the same—death.

Rick's sole hope was to reach the end of the corridor and await the alien soldier behind the building. Sucking in a deep breath, he focused on that thought. His long legs pumped out in quick sprinter's strides, carrying him toward his goal.

Pain!

A lash of fiery agony slashed across his right thigh. One of the beams had grazed his leg!

Groaning, he fought against a wave of torturous pain that swelled to engulf him. He staggered and stumbled. His shoulder slammed into solid wood that gave way beneath his weight, not shattering but swinging inward.

A door! His brain managed to recognize that he had fallen through a side doorway into the hangar itself.

Shifting the Uzi to his left hand, he clutched his thigh with the right and dragged himself through swirling pain and the hangar's interior darkness. And walked straight into a barrier of cold, hard metal.

This time his brain took what seemed like hours to focus and recognize the fact that he had collided with an airplane—a big one. Rick gritted his teeth to fight back the searing agony consuming his right leg, leaned against the metallic fuselage, and used it to guide him forward.

His left shin slammed into a metal ramp—no ladder! He reached up, his heart doubling its runaway pace. The plane's hatch was open.

Amid curses and groans, he found a rung of the ladder and pulled himself up into the plane's belly. He felt rather than saw the cardboard boxes stacked within the aircraft. A narrow path opened between the containers to his left. He pulled himself into it, then lay on his back with the Uzi pointed upward to meet the attack he knew would eventually come.

Outside he heard footsteps—the shock trooper came to claim victory.

Rick grimaced as he reached out with his right hand and found a handhold on the boxes. At least ten rounds remained in his clip. That was enough to take the snake with him. He pulled upward to brace himself against the boxes.

His right thigh brushed the containers. Waves of fresh agony swelled, washing over him, dragging him down into a churning maelstrom of blackness.

No! I won't die like this! he railed as unconsciousness swallowed him.

Chapter 2

Garth removed the dark sunglasses that protected eyes never meant to endure the harshness of Earth's yellow sun. For several silent moments he rubbed at the corners of his eyes with his good right hand, attempting to relieve the constant itching. Even after all these long months, he had not grown accustomed to the human-imitating lenses he wore.

Blinking several times to readjust the cosmetic lenses, Garth stared down at the dead stump that had once been his left hand. A smile that contained no trace of warmth curled his lips. If all went as he planned, he would soon permanently remove the irritation of these foolish lenses and revenge himself on the one who had cost him his hand.

As well as assuring my promotion to the commander of the invasion fleet! His smile widened to a grin, but the expression remained devoid of warmth.

Garth's gaze rose to the one-way mirror he stood before. On the opposite side of the glass wall, a young human female sat nude on an examination table. New life growing within her womb swelled her pink belly like a ripe, summery melon.

"Are you certain, Yvonne?" Garth asked, trying to imagine another human female, the woman who had burned away his hand, sitting on the table, her stomach bloated with child—his child!

"As I've assured you since we began this experiment

two months ago, I've duplicated Diana's efforts." A silky-haired brunette stepped beside Garth and peered coldly through the one-way mirror. "The fetuses are mature. The human cow will give birth before the week is out. You will have your star children."

"I will have the way to conquer this world," Garth said simply.

Yvonne's almond-shaped eyes shifted to the commander of the Houston Mother Ship. "Are you certain a hybrid is the key you seek?"

"Yes," he answered, his voice containing a certainty lacking in his mind.

Yet the genetic-engineered hybrid of human and Visitor had to be the key. Why else would the fleet's Scientific Commander Diana have produced Elizabeth Maxwell in the first place, were it not for the power she expected to unleash to aid her in crushing Earth? And why else would the ambitious bitch expend so much energy in trying to steal the star child from the humans, were it not for the same reason?

"I am not so certain, Garth." Yvonne shook her head and looked back at the human female who carried the seed of her experiment. "We are faced with too many unknowns. Two fetuses have developed in our subject. Even simple sonic scans reveal that our genes are dominant in one, while the human genes dominate the other. Everything indicates the same was true with Diana's own experiment. If so, what happened to the Visitor-dominant child?"

"Perhaps the humans butchered it," Garth replied, studying the determined set of Yvonne's oval face. "After all, Robin Maxwell gave birth after her escape from Diana's Mother Ship."

He paused and looked back at the human female. "However, the answers to your questions will have to wait. I want this woman and the life she carries in her belly destroyed."

"Destroyed?" Yvonne's head jerked around. Her eyes went saucer wide, then narrowed to slits.

"I have no further use for this female. Have her killed," Garth said. "I want it done before I fly north to Dallas."

"But the children she carries—aren't they what we've been working for these past two months?" Yvonne's voice rose an octave as she spoke. "How can you order her killed? How can you waste what I have given you?"

"She has served her purpose, proven that you can duplicate Diana's efforts." Garth turned away from his science officer. "But this woman will not mother my star child, nor shall some nameless soldier father it. The key I seek will be of my own blood, Yvonne. A child of my own flesh will lead us to victory."

"A child of your own flesh." Yvonne's voice quavered as she repeated his words. "Garth, what are—"

"Order this woman executed, Yvonne!" Garth pivoted and glared at his companion. "Do it now. I want her and the life she carries burned to a crisp. I want no trace to remain of her. Do you understand that?"

Yvonne nodded hesitantly, but said, "As you wish, Garth."

"Then do it now," he replied. "I will be here watching to make certain my orders are carried out."

Without another word Yvonne turned and walked from the small office. When the door closed behind her, Garth's gaze shifted back to the examination room on the other side of the mirror.

A minute later the door to the examination room opened and two shock troopers entered. The human female didn't even have time to scream before the soldiers unleased their weapons on her vulnerable body.

Garth smiled. Yvonne had been right; the woman's death was a waste. The young female would have made a nice main course for dinner that evening.

Chapter 3

A cloud of bothersome gnats swarmed about Rick Hurley's head. Lifting both arms, he swatted at the pesky insects.

In midair the gnats changed into hornets. Their droning roared in his ears as they dived around his head.

No! Rick refused to accept the abrupt metamorphosis.

In the next instant he sat in an empty roller coaster car as it hurled head-on down a hundred-foot drop.

No! Again Rick's brain rejected the sensations bombarding it. Gnats grown to hornets, roller coasters magically appearing from thin air—they simply could not be.

Unless— Cold sweat prickled over the young freedom fighter's body. He had heard of the horrors the lizards visited upon those they selected for mind molding. —*I'm in a conversion chamber!*

Swallowing the scream of panic that pushed its way up his throat, Rick struggled past the vision of the hurling roller coaster. Darkness swirled about him, then shattered into splintered fragments when he jerked his eyes open.

He stared up the side of a skyscraper of cardboard boxes. He blinked; the wall of brown corrugated containers remained. His right hand lifted, fingers testing the solid, unyielding surface of the boxes.

Real? Rick's brow knitted. More confusing than the

16

disturbing dream were the neatly stacked boxes that towered on each side of him.

The deafening drone—it still filled his ears.

How?

He rolled to the right in an attempt to sit. Pain burned through his thigh, and he remembered!

"Damn!" he cursed aloud and groaned as he sank to his back. The Visitor trap at the airport, the energy bolt grazing his leg, the hangar and the plane in which he had taken refuge—all came rushing back into his mind.

At that very instant the floor beneath him bucked. And again.

He groaned with the realization of what had given birth to his dream insects and roller coaster. The airplane he had hidden in was now airborne!

"Son of . . ." He muffled the rest of the curse. His head cocked from side to side. Another sound moved within the constant drone of the aircraft's engines— footsteps! They came toward him.

Ignoring the fiery pain awakened with each twist of his body, his arms groped around him, hands searching for the Uzi he had clasped when he had passed out.

Gone! My gun's gone!

"Well, I see you finally woke up. We were wonderin' if you'd decided to sleep until Judgment Day. You've been out for the long side of six hours now."

Rick's head twisted around. A tall, statuesque, flaming-haired angel dressed in khaki coveralls hovered over him. An ivory smile moved across an oval face lightly dusted with a sprinkle of fading freckles. Deep emerald eyes flashing an impish sparkle met his.

"Beautiful." The word slipped from his lips as though it had been uttered by a man in shock.

The coverall-clad angel's smile widened to a grin, and she chuckled. "A few fellows have told me the same thing. However, they were a mite more enthusiastic in their delivery."

The fiery-haired beauty slipped an olive-drab pouch off her shoulder and knelt beside Rick. "Of course, that was usually with a big ol' yellow moon overhead and the ulterior motive of lullin' my feminine defenses and lurin' me into a quick session of backseat bingo."

Rick continued to stare like a man in a trance. He had expected to be greeted by helmeted Visitor shock troopers. Instead, an angel had been sent to rescue him.

The silky strands of her shoulder-length hair swayed gently when she tilted her head to one side and eyed Rick's wounded thigh. "That line didn't work with red-blooded, healthy young jocks. For a man who tried to get his leg burned off, you'll have to come up with something a mite more original, Surfer Boy."

Rick blinked and shook his head. For the first time he noticed the young woman's accent, a slightly nasal twang that was somewhere between Old South Belle of the Ball and Southwestern Rodeo Queen. He smiled, his eyes never leaving that beautiful face.

"An angel with a southern accent." It was his turn to chuckle. "I passed out in the middle of a nightmare and I've woken up in the middle of a situation comedy."

"Watch your own mouth, friend. There's not a bit of the South in these words. It's all bred, born, and raised Texan." The redhead flashed Rick a mock scowl, then grinned widely. "Now if you'll scoot down my way a tad, I'll take a good look at that leg the snakes tried to shoot off."

Rick did as she suggested. The young beauty gingerly lifted a scorched flap of his blue jeans and studied the wound beneath. She pursed her lips and shook her head before her emerald-hued eyes returned to the resistance fighter.

"I know you were expectin' to take your insurance company to the cleaners over this, but I'm afraid I have to disappoint you. I've seen people come off the beaches in Galveston with worse burns than you're sportin'."

She opened the pouch, extracted a pair of scissors, and widened the rent in his pants an additional two inches. "You have a name?"

"Richard Hurley."

He grimaced when he glimpsed the wound the Visitor's energy bolt had left. To him, it looked far nastier than a sunburn.

"Most people call me Rick."

"Rick, mine's Sheryl Lee—Sheryl Lee Darcy." She pulled a tube of burn jelly from the pouch and spread a cool, clear layer of the disinfectant-smelling goop over the wound. "I was taught you weren't supposed to bandage a burn, but I think we need to give this a little protection and help keep it clean."

From the first-aid kit she produced a self-adhesive pad and lightly covered the wound. "That should be loose enough to let it breathe. Now let's see if we can get you on your feet."

"My feet?" Rick made no attempt to hide his doubt when Sheryl Lee stood and held out a helping hand. "You sure about this?"

"It's more comfortable up front, and Joe Bob wants to meet you." She snapped her fingers and impatiently straightened her arm. "Besides, you'll be wantin' to give your thank-yous to Joe Bob. He took care of the Visitor that followed you into the hangar last night."

Rick had forgotten the shock trooper who had followed him into the darkness. "I guess I do owe this Joe Bob a thank-you." He accepted Sheryl Lee's hand, and her fingers closed around his with surprising strength.

"I'll pull on three," she said. "One . . . two . . . *three!*"

With Sheryl Lee tugging and Rick pushing, they managed to get him to his feet with a minimum of groans and curses. He took a tentative step with his right leg, winced as pain flared anew through the thigh, and stood there swaying.

Sheryl Lee wrapped an arm around his waist. "Lean on me until you get your legs back. I don't want to pick you up from the floor again."

Without protest Rick slipped an arm around the redhead's waist. He smiled. The coveralls were loose and the firm form he felt beneath the khaki hinted of shapely feminine curves.

"I admit this is awful cozy, but the idea is to get you to the cockpit." Sheryl Lee flashed another of her ivory smiles and tilted her head forward. "Time to walk."

Rick grimaced and cursed when he placed his weight on the wounded leg. Sheryl Lee ignored the protest and edged him forward. By the sixth step Rick walked on his own with his redheaded nurse standing beside him with open arms to catch him should he falter.

"More stiff than painful," he admitted after another six steps. It was only a half lie. The burn did hurt, but he could almost ignore the pain—almost.

Slowly, cautiously, with Sheryl Lee ever ready in case he fell, they managed to squeeze their way between the secured stacks of cardboard boxes lining the length of the plane. Reaching the front of the craft, Rick glanced inside. Predawn grays and purples filled the windows that stretched above the lights of the plane's control panels.

A door had once separated the cockpit from the rest of the plane. The rusty remnants of hinges Rick noticed as he ducked through the doorway suggested that decades had passed since they last had served a useful function.

"So our stowaway finally decided to join us," a deep voice, as thickly accented as Sheryl Lee's, drawled when the two maneuvered through the low doorway.

"Name's Joe Bob Wills." The cockpit's sole occupant swiveled in the pilot's seat and extended a large-knuckled hand the size of a small island in Rick's general direction. "Named after my daddy and momma's favorite musician, the King of Western Swing himself, Bob Wills.''

Rick accepted the pilot's hand, shook it, and mumbled his own name, uncertain what the man was talking about or what to make of the aircraft's pilot.

The man's faded khaki jump suit might have been a twin to the one Sheryl Lee wore. Skull-tight, a worn and cracked aviator cap, complete with goggles resting on the forehead, nestled atop Joe Bob's head and drooped over his ears. A forest of salt-and-pepper hair pushed from under the edges of the cap to blend with another hairy forest bushed over the bottom part of the man's face.

Rick estimated the pilot's age in the late thirties or early forties. Yet he could not push aside the thought that Joe Bob appeared to be a geriatric case escaped from a 1960s love-in.

Releasing his stowaway's hand, Joe Bob Wills lifted a long, lanky arm and waved around the cockpit in a gesture that ended with him pointing at Sheryl Lee. "And this is my li'l' darlin' *Wanda Sue*."

"Wanda Sue?" Rick's gaze shot to the redhead; his forehead furrowed, questioning.

"He means the plane, not me. Joe Bob never loved a woman for more than one night," Sheryl Lee said as she slipped into the co-pilot's seat. "No woman could ever compete with this damned ol' airplane."

"What sweeter lover could a man ask for than a grand ol' lady like my *Wanda Sue*!" Joe Bob grinned widely and motioned Rick to a navigator's seat behind Sheryl Lee. "She wheezes a mite sometimes, and she coughs and spits. And on occasion she been known to leak at her seams. But, Lord, they don't make 'em like the C-47 anymore!"

C-47! Rick swallowed. He remembered building a plastic model of the Douglas-constructed transport while in his early teens. The twin-engine airplane hadn't been in production for over three decades! It had earned its claim to fame in World War II during the Normandy invasion, and later in 1948 during the Berlin airlift.

He swallowed again, hard. Fear prickled along his spine; his stomach did a sickly flip-flop. Worse, he was suddenly acutely aware of the aircraft's constant uneven vibration. He was flying in an antique, a relic of an age when jets seemed like science fiction. And in the pilot's seat was some aging hippie dressed like the Red Baron!

"I have to thank you and your friends for giving us cover last night," Joe Bob said over the roar of *Wanda Sue*'s dual engines. "Sheryl Lee and I had been sittin' in that hangar back at John Wayne for two days, right under the snakes' noses. Hell, we were sure they'd find us—and our cargo—any moment. If you and the others hadn't provided a diversion, we might never have gotten out of there."

"I'm glad we helped someone." Rick bit at his lower lip and drew a calming breath before giving the two a thumbnail sketch of the Visitor trap they had walked into the previous night. "Mind if I ask what cargo is so important to risk your necks on a night flight out of the L.A. area?"

"Drugs," Joe Bob answered.

"Drugs?" Rick's head snapped around. He couldn't believe he'd heard the man correctly.

"Drugs," Sheryl Lee repeated, her angelic smile beaming.

"The whole damned world is at war and you're smuggling drugs?" Rick tried to contain himself, but he couldn't. He exploded. "What are you carrying back there? Panama Red? Colombian coke? Or maybe you've got heroin. Jesus! I can't believe this! Nazi lizards from outer space are overrunning this planet, every one of them eyeing us like we were grade A prime ribs, and you two are flying drugs into Dipstick, Texas. This can't—"

"Dallas," Sheryl Lee cut in. Her eyes narrowed to

fiery points of green. An Arctic cold front howled in her voice when she spoke again. "We're flyin' into Dallas."

"Don't get riled, honey. The boy's made an honest mistake." Laughing, Joe Bob reached out and patted Sheryl Lee's shoulder. "*Wanda Sue* and me have made more than one low run across the Mexican border with Mary Jane as a passenger." The pilot glanced at Rick and winked. "However, this time we're strictly legit. Nothing but legitimate pharmaceuticals in those boxes."

"Antibiotics and medical supplies for Dallas and Fort Worth. We took these from a L.A. warehouse three nights ago," Sheryl Lee added, icicles still dripping from her words.

Rick's gaze rolled to the floor of the C-47 in embarrassment. He had read about the medical-supply theft in the newspapers. The Visitors had, of course, blamed the break-in on the Los Angeles resistance. At least they had gotten the resistance part correct, although they missed the city and state by about fifteen hundred miles.

"The Dallas–Fort Worth Metroplex is in dire need of any and all medicine they can get their hands on," Sheryl Lee continued.

"All of Texas is," Joe Bob added as he glanced at *Wanda Sue*'s instruments. "The Visitors have hit us pretty hard. Ain't like it is in Los Angeles. A Texan would rather bed down with the devil himself before he'd play house with the snakes."

The last remark jabbed at Rick like a finely pointed needle. Los Angeles with its provisional government must appear like a city of traitors to the rest of the country, he thought. "I guess I jumped to a hasty conclusion. How bad is it in your part of the country? The only contact we have with the rest of the world is the World Liberation Front and what we see on the Freedom Network."

"This should give you an idea, Rick." Joe Bob waved

him forward, then pointed to the cockpit window on his left. "Take a gander down there."

Rick ignored his throbbing thigh as he scooted behind the pilot's seat and craned his neck to see below. Rose and gold light of a new morning bathed the endless miles of flat farmland that stretched beneath the transport plane. "All I see is . . ."

He swallowed the remainder of his sentence. The shattered remains of what had once been a city slid into view. A network of streets and avenues was discernible amid the rubble of buildings and homes. Here and there the twisted frameworks of structures pushed toward the sky like tortured skeletons of steel.

"It has a name—or had one," Joe Bob said. "Lubbock, Texas. It once claimed to be the hub of the southwest plains. That was before the lizards paid it a visit."

Rick's gaze searched the ruins for any sign of life; he saw none—only destruction. Wide swaths of black ran through the debris, testimony to the Visitors' energy weapons and their awesome power.

"Why here?" Rick asked, unable to drag his eyes from the horror below. "I've never even heard of Lubbock before."

"There was an air force base just outside the city," Sheryl Lee explained. "The snakes couldn't tolerate a human military base so close to the edge of their free zone. When they hit, they destroyed the whole city to make an example of it for the rest of Texas."

Rick was familiar with the "free zone" the redhead mentioned. Los Angeles was within the zone. When the resistance had released the red bacterial toxin into the earth's atmosphere, it had driven the Visitors from the world. However, the toxin needed a sustained period of cold to reproduce. In the tropics and the subtropical areas of the world, the poison was totally ineffectual, creating a free zone where the Visitors could live without harm.

The majority of Texas was in that zone, and under alien control.

"Believe it or not, there's people still alive down there," Joe Bob said. "They're tryin' to rebuild a part of what they once had. To the north, in the panhandle, it's even worse."

"North?" Rick turned from the window as the *Wanda Sue* flew eastward, leaving the Lubbock ruins behind. "What's in the north?"

"Amarillo used to be," Sheryl Lee answered as Rick returned to the navigator's seat. "Every nuclear warhead in the United States was assembled in Amarillo. You might have seen the piece they did about it on television a few years back."

Rick shook his head. All he knew about Amarillo, Texas, was that it was mentioned in Chuck Berry's rock and roll classic "Route 66."

"The Visitors sure as hell couldn't leave that much human power layin' around." Joe Bob eased the nose of the airplane downward. "Amarillo's nothing but a cinder now. Another example of what the Visitors intend for the human race."

Rick's chest heaved as he sucked in a long breath, then let it escape through his teeth in a disgusted hiss. He had thought the Visitor suppression in Los Angeles was bad. Los Angeles hadn't even glimpsed the atrocities the snakes were capable of committing.

"It's been bad for most Texas cities." Sheryl Lee stared out the front of the plane for several moments before beginning again. "Most major Texas cities were home to military bases. San Antonio, Fort Worth, Houston, Corpus Christi, Killeen—the Visitors struck and struck hard. Opposition had to be eliminated fast."

"And the snakes play dirty." Joe Bob kept the *Wanda Sue* in a steep downward glide. "They've tried to blast us back into the Stone Age."

"You're not going to land us down there in the middle

of nowhere, are you?" Rick's gaze focused outside the plane on the desolate plain that seemed to be rushing up to meet them.

"Don't you worry about *Wanda Sue* or me none." Joe Bob chuckled. "We've both flown low enough to cut the tops off of cactus and managed to fly another day. I'll level off at fifty feet or so."

"We're inside the Visitors' strike perimeter," Sheryl Lee said, turning back to their passenger. "The only way to slip by the lizards is to come in low and fast to avoid their radar, or whatever they use instead of radar. We've got another two hours before we reach Dallas."

The altimeter dipped to thirty feet before Joe Bob leveled the ancient transport. Rick glanced from the window. The flat, featureless plain still raced by below the craft.

"Dallas . . ." Rick started, "is Dallas as bad as Lubbock?"

Sheryl Lee nibbled at her full lower lip and nodded. "It used to be a city of gleamin' glass and steel skyscrapers. Now it's mostly debris. Some of the residential areas and the suburbs haven't been hit as hard. But Dallas and Forth Worth are sittin' right on the boundary of the free zone. There were too many people in the Metroplex for the Visitors to let the cities just sit there."

"Fort Worth was hit harder. There was a Strategic Air Command base there." Joe Bob explained that Fort Worth was situated thirty-five miles west of Dallas and that sprawling suburbs connected the two Texas urban centers.

The two then outlined resistance efforts to shuttle residents north into Oklahoma and other states still protected by the Visitor-killing bacteria. It was a task that became increasingly dangerous with alien squad vehicles constantly patrolling the skies above the sister cities.

"Still, we manage to get carloads out every night,"

Sheryl Lee said. "It's not many people, but each man, woman, or child we run north is one less the lizards can butcher."

"Meanwhile, you've got to keep the ones still in the cities alive." Rick nodded his head toward the back of the plane and the boxes of medical supplies stacked there. "It sounds like an ambitious project."

"You've got a talent for understatin' the obvious," Joe Bob answered with a shake of his head.

"But it's workin'," Sheryl Lee pressed, hope filling her words. "All we need is time. In another six months we can evacuate the whole Metroplex. That's what the resistance is fighting for—time. One day we might be able to fight for our cities. For now, we just want time to save our people."

Rick shook his head and smiled sheepishly. "And I thought you were running coke and heroin."

Sheryl Lee shrugged. Her lips opened, but she never got the chance to speak.

"Sheeeiit!" Joe Bob's drawl dragged a simple one-syllable curse into three syllables.

Rick and Sheryl Lee turned to the pilot.

"Trouble, my friends," Joe Bob hissed through gritted teeth. "Comin' at us smack dab out of the sun!"

Rick glanced up and squinted as he peered out of *Wanda Sue*'s cockpit into the dawn. Nothing! He couldn't see anything but a blazing, yellow autumn sun.

A bolt of sizzling blue-white burst from the middle of the fiery orb. Rick's heart tripled its pace. The blast of energy ripped through the sky and sliced harmlessly past, mere feet above the C-47's right wing.

"Skyfighter!"

Sheryl's voice drew Rick's attention back to the nose of the plane. The source of the energy bolt was now visible—the blunt-nosed, compact form of a Visitor combat craft.

"What kind of ordnance are you carrying, Joe Bob?"

Rick asked with the sudden realization the subject had gone unmentioned.

"This." The pilot reached under his seat and a second later tossed Rick the missing Uzi. "And the forty-five I've got strapped to my waist."

"What? You're flying this old crate without any defense?"

Joe Bob jerked the transport's controls to the left as another beam of energy flared from the skyfighter's snout. The blast cut the air beneath the plane's rising wing.

"*Wanda Sue* was designed for haulin' cargo, not combat." Joe Bob reversed his maneuver, swinging his ponderous metallic lover to the south in time to dodge a third bolt from the snakes' ship. "In this baby's heyday there were fighter escorts to protect her."

The Visitor fighter shot over the ancient World War II transport in the next instant. Rick's stomach sank. In a few seconds the skyfighter would swing about and fly up their tail. This wasn't World War II; there were no fighters escorting the rickety old war-bird.

Wanda Sue dipped and swerved beneath Joe Bob's guiding hands. A pulse beam of five energy bolts lanced by the plane's left wing and disappeared into the rising sun.

"Got to make it to the edge of the Caprock," Joe Bob managed to grunt while he swung the transport back to the north. "The canyons there might give us cover."

Caprock? Canyons? Rick had no idea what the aging hippie was talking about. Nor did he have time to question the pilot.

Wanda Sue lurched violently. From the corner of an eye, Rick saw three energy blasts tear into the tip of the plane's left wing. Shards of jagged metal ripped through the morning sky as the transport plunged toward the ground below.

Chapter 4

Garth savored a sense of self-satisfaction as the squad vehicle skimmed over the ruins of downtown Dallas. This was the first time he had actually visited the city since the armada of Mother Ships had returned to Earth.

The month of daily and nightly attacks he had ordered from the Houston Mother Ship had left the city's skyscrapers seared piles of shattered concrete, brick, glass, and steel. In truth, he realized, whether human cities were razed to the ground now or later didn't matter. All would eventually be removed when this water-rich world was conquered and the Great Leader came from the mother world to reign over his new domain.

The squad vehicle banked, and the pilot seated beside Garth motioned to the right with his head. "There is the sports stadium the humans call the Cotton Bowl. Dallas Processing Center One operated there—until last night."

Garth pulled his gaze from the still-smoldering jumble of blackened rubble at the center of the oval stadium. "I've seen enough, Sergeant. Proceed to the second processing center."

The squad vehicle banked and shot northwest over the city toward an abandoned speedway on the edge of Dallas' northern suburbs. There Visitor teams still worked around the clock processing human captives for transport to the Mother Ships, where they would be placed in cold storage until there was need of their body protein.

Surely they must know it is futile, yet still they fight! Garth's self-pleased smile faded. How many ships had he sent against the Dallas–Fort Worth region? He had lost count of the numbers over the past months. *And still they fight!*

The stubbornness of the human mind eluded the Houston Mother Ship commander—especially these obstinate humans who called themselves Texans! Once under torture, an old, gray-haired man had spat into his face and shouted, "Remember the Alamo!" before his death screams had filled the interrogation chamber.

The Alamo? Garth was still uncertain of the significance of this Alamo. The human captives he had questioned since had only smiled and said that Texans would always remember the Alamo.

And that made even less sense to the Houston Mother Ship commander. After all, the humans themselves had destroyed the old mission when his troopers had retaken the city of San Antonio. Of what significance could there be in remembering a pile of blasted stone?

Garth's eyes drifted to the stump that ended his left arm. His surgeons had offered to replace the missing hand with a bionic transplant. He had refused. The missing hand was a constant reminder of a mistake he had once made—underestimating the determination and bestial desire for survival that burned in the human breast.

It had been in this very city, during the Visitors' first appearance on Earth, that he had lost his hand. Ten humans, including the female leader of Dallas' resistance, had been captured in an attack on Visitor Security Headquarters. Garth had chosen to personally interrogate the human bitch.

Even now he was not certain how the fiery-haired female managed to liberate the pistol from the holster on his hip and turn it to him. His laughter mocking her futile efforts had cost him a left hand—neatly burned away at the wrist by his own weapon—that day. The bitch not only freed herself from security headquarters, but took the rest of the conspirators with her.

Since that day, Garth had never underestimated the consuming willpower of his human enemies. Nor had he forgotten the redheaded she-demon who had robbed him of a hand.

The smile crept back to the corners of Garth's human-disguised mouth. Until now the means to repay the bitch in full had not existed. Yvonne's duplication of Diana's experiments with humans and Visitor genetic engineering had placed the tools of his long-dreamed revenge in his hands.

The bitch demon-spawn will pay. Oh, yes, she will pay dearly! The satisfaction that viewing the Cotton Bowl had leached from his spirits gradually returned to warm him.

The woman would not only bear the humiliation of serving those she fought against, but her womb would give birth to the child who would lead Garth's forces to victory.

My child—and hers! The sweetness of his scheme was intoxicating! His head reeled with drunken delight. *Oh, how the bitch will pay for all she did to me!*

"Commander," the pilot's voice intruded into Garth's euphoria, "we approach Dallas Processing Center Two."

Garth nodded. "Inform the center's commanding officer of our arrival and my desire to meet with him immediately."

"To meet with *her*," the sergeant corrected. "The base commander is female. She presently uses the human name Lisa."

"Whatever." Garth waved the pilot away and shook his head.

That was one problem with the Earth campaign over

which he had no control. The Great Leader placed far too
much weight on the abilities of simple-minded females.
All one had to do was look at how Diana had botched the
first invasion to see his point. Yet that damnable
scientific commander was still allowed to retain her
authority over the fleet.

Garth gnashed his dual set of reptilian teeth. There
were some things a career man had to endure for his
Leader and race, no matter how trying they were.

The white laboratory rat wiggled and squirmed, pink
feet vainly clawing the air as Garth held it in the air by its
tail. The Mother Ship commander tilted his head back.
He lifted the rat so that it struggled but an inch above his
face.

Gradually Garth's lower jaw extended, stretching the
elasticity of the human mask he wore to its limit. He
lowered the twisting rat into his gaping mouth and
carefully closed his jaw. With a small finger, he poked
the rodent's writhing tail between his lips and swallowed.

He felt his throat expand and constrict as his muscles
worked the still-struggling rat down into his stomach.
Lifting a hand to cover his mouth, he burped as politely
as possible.

"Thank you, Captain. A light snack was just what I
needed. I left Houston without breakfast this morning."
Garth eyed the two other rats waiting in a wire cage. For
a moment he considered popping both into his mouth,
then decided against the rodents. A large meal would
leave him lethargic, the one thing he didn't want to be
this day. Not with vengeance so near. "Have you
examined the photograph?"

"Yes, Commander Garth. This is the same woman
captured during the resistance raid last night." Lisa
handed the color glossy back to her superior officer.
"Are you certain you wouldn't prefer a meal that is a bit

more substantial? My chef is waiting to prepare you *anything* you might desire."

Garth waved away the offer, no matter how tempting it sounded. The "anything" to which Lisa referred was human flesh, of course. Those in the field were under strict orders only to capture and process human beings for future use. However, one of the benefits of being a field officer was that orders were often bent and eyes turned the other way.

"Perhaps another time, Captain, when I am not pressed by urgent matters," Garth said. "I came only for the woman today. May I see her now?"

"Of course. I've had her brought into the next room."

Lisa rose from her chair and pressed imagined wrinkles from her red uniform. The action did not go unnoticed. Garth silently admired the shapely curves over which the woman's hands slid. For an instant he pondered the real beauty that lay veiled beneath the mousy brunette disguise the captain wore. Perhaps when circumstances permitted him to accept Lisa's dinner invitation, he would have time to explore what he could only fantasize about now.

"This way, Commander." Lisa stepped to a door at the side of her office and held it open for him.

Garth rose and walked through the entrance. The room he entered was bare except for a sheet-covered table. Garth's eyes widened. Something lay beneath the white sheet draping the table.

"Captain, what is this?" Garth's head jerked around; he glared at Lisa. "I hope this isn't your idea of a joke."

"Joke?" Lisa's head shifted from side to side in befuddlement. "This is the woman you have been searching for."

"No! It can't be!" Garth strode to the table and tore back the sheet.

A constricted gasp pushed from his throat. It was the

redheaded bitch. It couldn't be, yet it was. And she was dead!

"What is this, Captain? Your message said that you had captured the human female!" Garth tossed the sheet back across the pale, lifeless form. "Now you give me this—a corpse!"

"The original communiqué told of the woman's capture and her wounds." Lisa's words quavered with fear. "My second message reported her death from those wounds."

"Second message . . ." Garth sputtered. He had received no second message. "There was no second message."

"It was sent an hour ago," Lisa answered.

"Damn!" Garth could not repress the reptilian hiss that spat from his human-disguised lips. An hour ago he had been en route from Houston to Dallas. The captain's message had not been relayed to him.

The taste of vengeance that had been honey sweet but moments ago turned bile bitter in his mouth. He had been robbed, his months of planning and scheming stolen from him.

"Commander, what would you like done with the body?" Lisa asked timidly.

"I could not care less, Captain. A corpse is of no use to me!" Garth pivoted and hastened from the empty room.

It can't end like this! Hate and anger railed through his head as he returned to the squad vehicle outside. *I won't be cheated! I won't be cheated!*

Chapter 5

"Hang on! One of these babies once flew the hump with half a wing missing!" Joe Bob's big-knuckled hands eased back on the controls. His right arm snaked out; fingers flipped and flicked a series of switches.

Rick's stomach lurched toward his throat. The C-47's ragged left wing lifted. Metal groaned in protest. A violent shudder shook the plane from nose to tail.

"What the hell was that?" Sheryl Lee's emerald eyes grew saucer wide.

Rick's own gaze darted about the cockpit; he expected to find portions of the instrumentation shaken off the hull. Another jarring shock wave quaked through the *Wanda Sue*'s ancient fuselage. Still the rickety transport stayed aloft and in one piece!

"Forget the vibrations. It's only the landing gear," Joe Bob drawled in an emotionless monotone reminiscent of that of an airline pilot. "Got to set us down. No way to outfly the snakes. *Wanda Sue* was never made for combat maneuvers."

A series of three additional teeth-rattling quakes jarred the transport. Rick's hands closed around the arms of the navigator's chair in a death grip. The man in the pilot's seat was insane. There was no way he could possibly land the plane here in the middle of this arid wasteland.

Outside, the flat, neatly furrowed farmland gave way to mesquite-sprinkled plains. Rick saw clumps of bushy growth one moment, and in the next the gnarled branches of the tough little trees loomed below.

"That's it, sweet thing, just lift your chin a little bit more. Bring your nose up, baby, and everything will be all right," Joe Bob crooned while he pulled the control stick back to his stomach. "That's it. That's it. I knew you had it in you. I knew it."

The stubby, rounded nose of the transport lifted. The whine of extending flaps pierced the rattle of constant vibrations shaking the plane. Abruptly the plane's nose shifted. Cloudless blue sky filled the cabin's windows.

Wanda Sue screamed, her metal struts and plates groaning in anguish as the landing gear slammed into the sandy soil. The ponderous transport bounced, then jarred back to the ground. Joe Bob's right hand found the engine control levers and threw the two prop-driven dynamos into reverse.

"All right, sweet thing! I knew you wouldn't let me down!" An ear to ear grin proudly beamed through the forestlike beard covering Joe Bob's face. "I knew you had it in—"

"Joe Bob, rocks!" Sheryl Lee's voice lacked the comforting drone of the pilot's; she screamed.

Rick's gaze jumped to the redhead just in time to see the C-47's right wing plow into an outcropping of yellow limestone. The world suddenly became a maelstrom.

Wanda Sue spun, careening wildly. Rich heard a landing strut snap beneath the plane. The transport swung about, spinning in the opposite direction as the ragged tip of its left wing gouged the sand.

Rick's viselike grip on the chair's arm was to no avail. Tumbling head over heels, he flew from the seat. He hit the floor of the cockpit and skidded right shoulder first into the bulkhead.

Above the whining cries of twisting metal, he heard Sheryl Lee scream. A second later she crashed atop him with arms and legs flailing the air.

Then *Wanda Sue* lay motionless. Only the sound of a West Texas wind came from outside. Inside, Rick and

Sheryl Lee groaned in harmony while they disentangled themselves from one another.

A flower of red blossomed at the center of the bandage on Rick's thigh; it was accompanied by a pulsing pain. Gritting his teeth, he carefully began to examine himself. His head and shoulder felt as though someone had taken a sledgehammer to them. Several cuts and scrapes welled crimson on the backs of his hands, and bruises too numerous to count ached on chest, back, arms, and legs, but there were no broken bones. Somehow he managed to come through the whirlwind landing in one piece.

"I seem to be all here," Sheryl Lee said incredulously, her eyes rising to Rick. She looked like he felt, yet managed a smile, weak but still radiant. "I think the old saying is, 'Any landing you can walk away from is a good landing.' Hey, Joe Bob?"

There was no answer.

The two looked at the pilot's seat. Joe Bob lay slumped over the controls of his winged lover.

"God, no. No." Tears welled from Sheryl Lee's eyes and trickled down dirt-smudged cheeks.

Were it not for the grotesque, twisted angle of his neck, Rick would have thought the pilot had simply leaned forward in the seat and closed his eyes. The landing had been bad for Joe Bob Wills. The man would not walk away from *Wanda Sue* this time. He and his airborne lover had died in each other's arms.

"How?" Sheryl Lee turned to Rick. "We're both alive. How could he be dead? How?"

Rick's head moved slowly from side to side. He reached out and held the trembling woman. "I think we'd better get out of here. There could be a fuel leak."

Sheryl Lee wiped at her eyes, sniffed, and nodded. Finding the Uzi on the opposite side of the cockpit, Rick hefted it in his left hand, then used his right to help the redhead from the floor. Together they worked their way over scattered boxes of medical supplies to the back of the plane. To Rick's surprise, the door swung outward, opening without resistance. A hot Texas autumn wind raked at their faces when they stepped outside.

The hiss of discharge energy crackled in the air! Blue-white bolts sizzled into the sand ten feet from where they stood. Sand fused to glass under the intense heat of the beam.

"Sons of bitches!" Rick's head jerked up.

The Visitor skyfighter hovered five hundred feet in the air above them. Another burst of crackling energy flared from its blunt snout, slamming into the ground five feet closer than the first bolt.

"The rocks! Run!" Rick shoved Sheryl Lee toward the outcrop that had so abruptly ended *Wanda Sue*'s landing. "Get to cover!"

Swinging the Uzi's muzzle skyward, he squeezed the trigger. The clip's remaining ten shots spat from the pistol in a deafening bark. The skyfighter swerved, banking to the left. Digging a hand into a jacket pocket for another clip, Rick sprinted after Sheryl Lee.

They had covered half the distance to the rising crag of rock before a high-pitched whine announced the skyfighter's approach. From out of the north the sleek white craft dived. Actinic light spat from the alien craft's nose.

Grasping the young woman's arm, Rick wrenched her to the left. Energy bolts like strafing machine-gun bullets sizzled into the sand where they had stood but a fraction of a second before.

Rick snapped the fresh clip into the Uzi and sprayed twenty rounds after the retreating ship. The ammunition and effort were wasted. The skyfighter banked and came soaring back for another run at the fleeing humans.

"Zigzag!" Rick shouted and once more pushed Sheryl Lee toward the protection of the limestone outcropping.

Meanwhile, he pulled out another clip and jammed it into the Uzi. Legs wide in a stance of defiance, he lifted the machine pistol and carefully aimed at the incoming craft. His finger curled around the trigger, and he waited, sweat beads popping out on his forehead.

The Visitor ship dipped lower, riding just above the southern horizon. The familiar glare of blue-white light burst from its nose. Sand and flame erupted from the earth as the deadly bolts ripped into the ground. Closer the strafing shafts of power raced on a direct line toward the lone man.

Rick's trigger finger tensed.

The roar of machine guns filled the air. The skyfighter abruptly pulled up and veered to the east.

Rick stared in disbelief. He hadn't fired a shot!

The thunder of unbridled mechanical horsepower screamed overhead. The reflection of sunlight on naked metal momentarily blinded Rick's eyes as he looked up. He blinked away the glare and stared above once again. His disbelief tripled.

"Surfer Boy, get the hell out of there!"

Sheryl Lee's warning cry brought him to life. He raced to where she waited by the limestone before staring back at the sky. The flashing silver form remained, trailing the skyfighter.

"Has the whole damned world gone mad?" Rick still could not accept what he saw. "Do you know what that is?"

"An airplane," Sheryl Lee answered simply.

"It's a Mustang—a P-51!"

"So?"

Overhead the skyfighter soared in a tight loop. The metal plane hung right on the ship's tail like a shark of the skies.

"That thing's as old as *Wanda Sue*! It's a World War II bomber escort! Perhaps the finest prop fighter the U.S. ever made!" Rick watched the Mustang follow the Visitor craft through a series of rolls. He told himself it was impossible, but another of those plastic models he had built as a teenager had suddenly come to life.

The old fighter stuck to the alien ship. Now and then fire flared from the wings of the streamlined fighter and the staccato bark of six 50mm machine guns rolled from the sky.

Mouth agape, Rick's eyes followed the two aircraft through the cloudless Texas sky. The compact skyfighter rolled, looped, dived, and soared. As though it were tied to the snakes' ship by some invisible line, the Mustang matched every evasive maneuver, its single engine roaring.

Dogfights like this just didn't happen anymore, except in war movies. Rick knew that were it not for the fact that one of the ships had come across the galaxy from the fourth planet of the star Sirius, he might have been watching a reenactment of a battle first staged during World War II or the Korean War.

The skyfighter pulled out of an inverse loop and whined toward the limestone outcropping. Still glued to the Visitors' backside, the P-51 gracefully completed its own loop and opened up with its six wing machine guns again.

"He's got 'em!" Sheryl Lee's arms went around Rick's neck, hugging him in abandoned joy. "He's got 'em!"

A plume of greasy black smoke erupted from the tail of the skyfighter. The ship swerved from side to side. The Mustang matched every move with machine guns ablaze.

Abruptly, the Visitor ship dipped, diving toward the ground. It did not pull up from this maneuver but plowed into the earth a hundred yards from the crippled *Wanda Sue*.

"Down!" Rick pulled Sheryl Lee to the ground, covering her with his body. His own arm sheltered his head from the explosion he knew would come.

There was no blast. The skyfighter simply lay in the sand, black smoke pouring from its cracked hull.

Overhead the Mustang did a victory roll, banked eastward, and disappeared over the horizon.

Chapter 6

Rick ducked through *Wanda Sue*'s rear exit, holding a thermos half filled with coffee and a plastic milk bottle sloshing with water. Sheryl Lee sat in the shadow cast by one of the crumpled wings. He walked beside her and lowered himself to the sand. A sigh of relief slid from his lips as he stretched out his right leg.

"Still hurting?" the redhead asked without looking up.

"Some, but I can manage." He reached behind his back and pulled Joe Bob's .45 from his belt and nudged the young woman's shoulder. "You better take this. You might need it before we get out of here."

"Out of here?" She turned to him, doubt masking the lovely features of her oval face. "We aren't going anywhere. This plane's still filled with medical supplies I have to get to Dallas and Fort Worth. We can't leave them here in the middle of nowhere."

"We sure as hell can't carry them out of here on our backs," Rick replied with a shake of his head. "And we're not just waiting here until somebody comes along. Odds are that *somebody* will be big, nasty, green, and reptilian. The Visitors are going to miss that skyfighter and eventually send others out looking for it—if they aren't on the way already."

Sheryl Lee didn't answer. Her gaze returned to the sand at her feet.

"I found this in the cockpit. Can you point out where

41

we might be?" Rick pulled one of Joe Bob's charts from his jacket and opened it across his lap.

"We passed over Lubbock but hadn't left the Caprock." Sheryl Lee's fingertip found a black circle enclosing two parallel lines that represented what had once been Lubbock's airport. She traced eastward. "This is the edge of the Caprock. We're someplace in between."

"Caprock?" Rick lifted eyebrows.

"These flatlands are the top of the Caprock." She swept an arm before her. "The Caprock ends abruptly with an escarpmentlike drop that's eight hundred, maybe a thousand feet down to rugged country. It's still considered plains, but it ain't like any midwestern wheatfield plains you're used to seeing on television. It's red sand country. Nothing but wind and water-eroded gullies and ravines. It's good for growing prickly-pear cactus, mesquites, rocks, and more rocks."

"Not exactly hospitable sounding." Rick's attention returned to the chart. "What are these dots?"

Sheryl Lee shrugged. "Could be any of several small towns spread out in this area. Most of them are little more than a gas station and maybe a country store. The type of places you'd miss if you blinked while drivin' through."

"They sound like the type of places the Visitors would ignore. Too small to worry about." Rick pointed to a dot north of an imaginary line running eastward from Lubbock to the Caprock. "If we managed to make it halfway to this Caprock of yours, we should be relatively close to here."

"Close if you consider forty to sixty miles close," Sheryl Lee said without enthusiasm. "This country's like walking in the desert, Surfer Boy. Little or no water, and if we miss that town by even a fraction of a degree, then all we'll do is just keep walking to nowhere."

"There's got to be highways and farm roads, and they

have road signs." He pushed gingerly from the ground, trying not to wince as renewed pain shot through his thigh.

"Ranch roads," Sheryl Lee corrected. "You're in West Texas now; it's ranch roads."

"Farm, ranch—it doesn't matter as long as they're roads with signs." He reached down and helped her to her feet. "At least we won't have to contend with hills."

While she brushed the sand from the seat of her khaki coveralls, Rick surveyed the vast flatlands surrounding them. For miles and miles all he saw was miles and miles. His gaze came to rest on the wrecked skyfighter.

"It's stopped smoking." He nodded at the downed Visitor craft. "I want to take a look inside. With luck they were carrying side arms." He patted the pockets of his jacket. "I've only got a few more clips before this Uzi's useless."

Sheryl Lee waved for him to lead the way. With another nod Rick stepped across the sand to a crack twice his width that split the side of the skyfighter. He flicked the safety off on the machine pistol and poked his head inside.

The craft's white interior was now a smoky slate gray. Here and there an occasional light winked on the control panel, but for the most part the skyfighter's instruments appeared to be quite dead.

"There's a pilot and a co-pilot," he said to Sheryl Lee as she entered the craft. "Both are still in their seats. Better yet, they're both wearing energy pistols."

"Get 'em and let's get out of here." Sheryl Lee rubbed her hand over her arms and shivered in spite of the Texas morning heat. "It feels like we're entering a rattler pit."

"We're insulting Earth's reptiles by comparing them to these things," Rick said with a smile as he moved to the body of the Visitor in the co-pilot's seat. "Ugly bastards, aren't they?"

Sheryl Lee shivered again as her gaze shifted to the

extraterrestrial creatures that had piloted the skyfighter. Rick's own reaction was a disgusted grunt.

The human disguises the two aliens wore no longer concealed their reptilian faces. Torn and cracked in the crash, the plasticlike makeup dangled from forehead, cheeks, and chin. Beneath were faces that bespoke an evolutionary process far removed from the ancestral mammalian tree that gave rise to man.

The aliens' high protruding foreheads and thin noses with slitted nostrils were like something normally reserved for the blackness of human nightmares. Green scales, mottled with patches of black, covered the unearthly visages.

Rick gave silent thanks that the aliens' eyes had closed before they died. Those eyes were the invaders' most hellish feature—fiery orange orbs with black slits for pupils. They were the eyes of an alligator or crocodile except they were alive with a smoldering intelligence.

An involuntary shivery chill worked its way up the young man's spine. If their scientific and technological advances were an indication of their superior intelligence, the possiblity provided no relief from Rick's primal fear of them.

Reaching down, he unsnapped the holster of the alien in the co-pilot's seat and slipped a blue-black pistol from the scabbard. "You know how to work one of these?" He handed the weapon to Sheryl Lee.

The flaming-haired Texan hefted the awkwardly designed firearm, flicked a switch near its handle, then moved the priming lever back and forth several times. "Full charge and primed."

Rick pursed his lips thoughtfully. Sheryl Lee's graceful beauty was as deceptive as her charming accent. This was no pampered Southern belle, but a woman descended from strong pioneer stock. She displayed no awkwardness or hesitation with the weapon.

A trace of an amused smile moved over her red lips

when she noticed Rick's stare. "My daddy took me quail huntin' with him for the first time when I was five years old. I had my own twenty-two rifle by the time I was seven and a deer rifle at ten. I'm no stranger to rifles or pistols. This nasty little thing just fires a different type of bullet. Kind of like the snakes themselves, it hisses instead of giving a good healthy bark."

With a shrug Rick turned to the dead Visitor slumped in the pilot's seat. Sheryl Lee was far more familiar and at home with firearms than he. He had never even held a rifle or a pistol until the Visitors' first arrival on Earth.

The Uzi that was now his constant companion had only been an exotic ornament of spy novels before he joined the resistance. In fact, the first time he had actually seen one of the machine pistols was in the hands of Secret Service agents during the repeated television newscasts of the assassination attempt on President Ronald Reagan.

Opening the pilot's holster, he extracted the pistol and checked the charge and primer lever. Like Sheryl Lee's weapon, the energy gun carried a full charge and had not been damaged in the crash.

His gaze traveled around the interior of the skyfighter before returning to his companion. "I don't think there's anything else we can use here. Let's see if we can find that town now."

Sheryl Lee made no attempt to hide her relief when she turned and stepped from the crack in the downed craft's hull. Rick took two steps after her when he heard a rustling behind him. He started to look around.

A mountain of animated flesh—reptilian flesh— slammed into his side!

"Ooomph!" Air exploded from his lungs under the impact. The weight of his attacker sent him sailing through the ragged rent in the ship's side.

He hit the ground twisting, but the living mountain remained atop him, an oppressive weight that crushed down on his lungs, making it impossible to breathe. Fingers, cold, scaly, clawed fingers closed around his neck. Thumbs pressed into his windpipe.

Unable to think or focus, he balled his fists and struck out blindly. Again and again he hammered the blurred boulder of green and black that hovered above his head.

Spitting hisses answered his rain of blows. The ever-increasing pressure choking his throat lessened.

Rick threw his legs in the air and brought them down with all the strength he could muster. At the same time, his chest lurched upward and he twisted to the left.

The unnaturally cold alien hands slipped from his neck, the grip of the scaly claws broken. He lurched and twisted again, unseating the massive weight perched on his chest. Then he rolled free. Finding hands and knees, he scuttled through the sand while he sucked cooling air into his burning lungs.

"Rick, look out!"

He heard Sheryl Lee's warning, managed to turn and focus just before the lizard-faced monster plowed into him once more.

He groaned as the weight of the collision carried him to his back for a second time. Not waiting for the viselike hands to close around his throat, he swung at the Visitor's head.

The reptile's fingers snapped shut about his wrists. Like an adult holding the arms of a child, the alien pinned its human opponent's arms to the ground. Above Rick the corners of a lipless mouth curled back in a grotesque mockery of a human smile. That mouth opened and a blood-red forked tongue serpentinely writhed as the Visitor hissed its anger.

Repeating his earlier method of escape, Rick threw his legs in the air and lurched as he brought them down. He bucked and wrenched his body from to side to side. The reptilian nightmare remained firmly planted atop him.

Another resounding hiss spat from the scaled mouth.

With the tongue flicking like a lizard smelling the air, the alien's head slowly lowered. The tongue disappeared back into the Visitor's mouth, then in the next instant lashed out like a living bullwhip and wrapped itself about its victim's neck.

"Aarrraaarrrhhh." A strangled gasp gurgled from Rick's throat.

The nooselike tongue tightened, a garrote of alien flesh and blood that would complete the task the Visitor's thumbs had started.

Thrashing, kicking, lurching, Rick struggled to free himself. His head jerked from side to side in an attempt to loosen the closing ring of death that tightened about his neck with each passing second. It didn't help. He could dislodge neither the Visitor's weight nor the creature's hellish tongue as it gradually choked the life from his body.

A high-pitched whine cut through the rush of the West Texas wind. A flare of blue-white light glared behind the Visitor. The alien jerked upright, body rigid.

A heartbeat later the creature's choking tongue went flaccid, uncurling from Rick's neck. Atop the California freedom fighter, the Visitor jerked and twitched spasmodically before tumbling to the sand to lie there unmoving.

Above him Sheryl Lee stood with a Visitor energy pistol held stiff armed before her. The muzzle of the weapon shifted, keeping a steady aim on the alien for any sign it might still live.

"Thank you," Rick managed to gasp-mumble while he inhaled deep, cool lungfuls of air and exhaled. He pushed the Visitor's legs from him and stood, grateful that the young woman not only knew how to handle a gun, but knew how to use it as well.

"How could it still be alive?" The barrel of the energy pistol dipped, and Sheryl Lee's emerald eyes lifted to

Rick. "We're well north of the Visitors' free zone here. If the crash didn't kill it, then the red dust should have."

Rick's gaze moved back to the lizard man sprawled on the sand. Sheryl Lee was right; they were north of the free zone. He was so used to living in Los Angeles where the bacterial toxin had no effect on the Visitors that he hadn't considered a living alien anything out of the ordinary. Here the red dust should have killed the snake within seconds.

"I don't know." He arched an eyebrow. "Maybe it takes longer for the poison to work here so close to the free zone."

Sheryl Lee nibbled at her lower lip and shrugged. "I never heard anyone mention a slower reaction time before."

"Well, it sure as hell didn't knock him out immediately," Rick answered. "It's been at least a half hour since that Mustang brought down the skyfighter."

Rick pivoted and stared at the wrecked alien ship. "His friend!"

Without another word of explanation, Rick snatched his dropped energy pistol from the sand and darted back into the ship. A flare of harsh blue-white light accompanied by the crackling hiss of released energy preceded his exit from the craft.

"I made certain his friend wouldn't suddenly come back to life," Rick answered Sheryl Lee's questioning gaze. "The last thing we need is the co-pilot radioing his position to his fellow snakes."

The coverall-clad redhead nodded.

Her reaction sent a chilling shudder through the Californian. The nod, the casual acceptance of his act, was like viewing a mirror reflection of himself. He had just placed the barrel of a gun to the head of a sentient creature and pulled the trigger. The war they fought defined the action as a matter of simple survival. Yet he could not escape the feeling he had acted as an executioner, not a soldier.

There should be guilt, a sense of loss, he told himself, trying to detect a hint of those emotions within him. He found them in neither himself nor the Texas beauty who lifted the water bottle and thermos from the ground. It was as though he had swatted an annoying insect rather than killed a sentient being.

He sucked at his teeth in disgust. At twenty-two life should only be filled with beauty, not hard, cold bitterness. The Visitors were robbing humankind of more than just their home world and their lives. They were gradually leaching away man's humanity.

"If we're goin' to find that town, we'd best be headin' out, Surfer Boy."

Sheryl Lee's voice brought him from his bitter reflections. He looked, smiled weakly, and started walking northward over the sandy flatlands.

Chapter 7

Rick Hurley's gaze scanned the country that swept north before them. In the five hours and estimated fifteen miles that had passed since they left the *Wanda Sue* behind, it had changed little. Wind-gnarled mesquite trees, an occasional scrub cedar, sand, rock, and flatness were all that met the eye.

A southern wind blew across this land Sheryl Lee called the *Llano Estacado*, the Staked Plains. Coming directly up from the Mexican deserts, the wind seared the skin like a blast from an open kiln.

Rick glanced at the unmerciful sun that scowled overhead. A few high feathery clouds wisped on the wind offered no hope of even a brief respite from the broiling heat.

"Must be ninety-five if it's a degree." He swiped at a sheen of sweat on his forehead with a forearm. The effort did nothing more than mingle the perspiration on his arm with that on his face. "And you people call this autumn? It's late September, for Chrissake!"

"Why do they still wear the human masks?" Sheryl Lee asked from out of the blue, as though she hadn't heard his complaints.

"What?" Rick glanced at the woman. Her khakis were unstained by even the slightest trace of sweat. "Masks?"

"The Visitors—why do they maintain their human charade? It doesn't make any sense. The whole world knows what they look like. Do they think we wake up each day and it's a whole brand-new world to us?" Her eyebrows dipped over her emerald eyes and her brow furrowed. "It really doesn't make any sense, does it?"

"I think the sun's getting to you more than it's getting to me. Your brain's slowly cooking. Why don't we take a breather?" Rick waved an arm toward the sand. One spot was just as good as the next. Shade was a rare commodity in this harsh country.

"It's too dry here to be hot. You want hot, then imagine these temperatures mixed with high humidity— that's Dallas," Sheryl Lee answered.

However, Rick noted the young redhead made no objection to his suggested rest. She sank to the sand, opened the water bottle, took a swig, then passed it to him when he lowered himself beside her.

The water was hot and tasted like plastic, but it was wet trickling down his parched throat. He was tempted to take another swallow but replaced the container's cap instead. Sheryl Lee had restricted herself to one sip; he could manage on the same amount.

"Why do you think the Visitors still wear their human makeup?" she rephrased her original question.

"Come to think of it, it really doesn't make much sense, does it?" He shrugged and glanced at her. "Why'd you bring it up?"

"Those two snakes in the skyfighter today with their masks ripped away just started me wonderin'." Sheryl Lee leaned back, supporting herself on her elbows. "The masks don't seem to make much sense anymore, not with the whole world knowin' what they look like."

Rick agreed, but in truth he had never thought about it before. The lizards had been unmasked, yet they still maintained their human disguises. "Maybe it's a matter of public relations."

"Huh?"

"Maybe they're trying to play with our minds. You

know, if they look like us, it will make them more acceptable in the long run—easier for us to deal with aliens that appear human. If they ran around looking like the snakes they are, it would be a constant reminder of the differences that exist between us. You have to admit it would be hard for Diana to convince the world she was all love and light if each time she went on television the world saw those damnable orange reptile eyes and watched her lizard tongue flicking the air."

Rick lifted a hand and rubbed at his neck. He could still feel the alien tongue that had wrapped itself about his throat like a noose.

"Maybe you're right, but I don't know." Sheryl Lee shook her head dubiously. "Surely they don't think we're that stupid. That we'd be taken in by a bit of powder and rouge."

Rick brushed back a strand of blond hair the wind tossed across his forehead. "I believe that's exactly what they think. They see themselves as creatures born to rule the universe, and we're merely cattle to be bred and slaughtered."

"Slaughtered," Sheryl Lee repeated with a shiver. "That's what they did to my father. He was a geologist caught up in the scientist conspiracy the Visitors foisted on the world when they first arrived. He was arrested, tried, and convicted on charges of conspiring with other scientists in a plot to horde oil supplies. That was here in Texas of all places, where oil's always been important to our economy!"

Rick saw the tears that welled and misted her green eyes, although her voice neither trembled nor quavered.

"Shock troopers shot him down as he was led from the courtroom," she continued. "They claimed he attempted to escape. It made good headlines for their propaganda machine. And believe me, it made every Texas newspaper and television channel."

Sheryl Lee paused and swallowed hard. She stared at

the horizon, her eyes never meeting Rick's. "That's when my mother and I joined the resistance. Lord, we thought we had won with the red dust. We thought we had won!"

Rick reached out and rested a hand on her shoulder. "I know. I was a student at UCLA when the Visitors first appeared. Like the rest of the world, I thought our saviors had arrived from the stars."

His chest constricted and his throat grew tight as memories he had tried to bury burst from their neat niches and flooded his mind. "My family—mother, father, and sister—lived in a small town on the coast north of Los Angeles. One night every resident in that town disappeared. They were there one day, then the next they were gone."

"Processed by the Visitors?" Sheryl Lee's gaze shifted to her companion.

"Yeah," Rick nodded. "Like canned meat, the Visitors stuffed them into those gelatin capsules and placed them in cold storage in a Mother Ship."

"Then there's a possibility they're still alive." Encouragement filled the redhead's voice.

"Perhaps. But I don't know which Mother Ship they were taken to." In Rick's voice there was only helplessness.

He knew the immensity of the Visitors' Mother Ships and their numbers. Each vessel had the capacity of storing millions of captives. To find his family would mean capturing the whole fleet of five-mile-diameter ships. Bringing the moon to the Earth would be a far easier task.

"We've both drawn a sorry hand from life," Sheryl said. "But those are the cards we've got to play with."

"And right now we still need to find a town . . ."

"Or a road," she concluded. "We don't want to be stuck out here tonight. It might be hot at the moment, but soon as the sun goes down, we'll both be shiverin'."

V

Pushing up from the ground, Rick stood, stretched, then offered the khaki-clad girl a hand. She accepted, pulling herself to her feet and unscrewing the top to the water bottle again.

"One for the road, Surfer Boy." She smiled, took a swig, and passed the plastic jug to Rick.

"Surfer boy?" He licked at his lips to moisten their cracking surface after wetting his mouth with another sip. "How in hell did you come up with that?"

"All you boys out in California are surfers, the way I hear tell," she answered as they resumed their northward trek.

He chuckled and shook his head.

"Come on, you can 'fess up. You have blond hair, a dark tan, and look muscled enough all over to fit the part." She grinned. "I can just see you ridin' the waves at Malibu or one of those beaches we're always hearing about."

"Actually, I've only been on a surfboard a few times in my life," he replied. "Tennis was my sport. Before the Visitors came I had hopes of eventually giving it a try on the professional circuit. Wasn't too bad a player in school."

Her smile widened to a grin. "Beach bum, tennis bum—same difference. California, land of the idle rich."

"I thought that was here in Texas? You know—cattle barons and oil millionaires everywhere you turn."

It was Sheryl Lee's turn to laugh. "Always wanted to be a poor little rich girl. But my momma and daddy didn't cooperate. Never could understand why, either."

"Maybe one of these days you'll—"

He didn't get a chance to finish his sentence. Sheryl Lee's arm shot out in front of his chest, halting him. As he glanced at her, he heard rather than saw the reason for her reaction. He turned to the right, seeking the source of the faint buzzing sound that whispered beneath the wind.

"God!" His eyes widened when his gaze alighted on the bundle of brown-and-black-mottled coils ten feet to his side.

"Yep." Sheryl Lee eased him away from the coiled snake. "That's a rattler."

"I didn't know they came in the two-headed variety." Rick watched the poisonous snake's twin heads weave slowly from side to side. Behind those heads a tail with two rattlers vibrated angrily.

"Don't usually," the redhead answered. "But ever since the red dust was released, there have been more and more weird creatures like that poppin' up in this part of the country."

"A mutation?" Rick cast the young woman a sideways glance as they circled the two-headed reptile, giving it wide berth. "But I thought the bacteria wasn't harmful to terrestrial life forms."

"It wasn't supposed to be." Sheryl Lee looked over her shoulder at the still-coiled rattlesnake, then proceeded northward at Rick's side. "Maybe once we released it in the atmosphere, it changed the way the virus did in that movie *Andromeda Strain*. But it's not just the rattlers that are affected. It's the coyotes, jackrabbits, prairie dogs—all the wildlife. I've heard reports of cows and horses suddenly gone sterile."

Rick listened, uncertain of what he heard. If the red dust humankind had used to combat the Visitors was causing the mutations, then the biological weapon was as dangerous to Earth's denizens as it was to the alien invaders. And without the red dust, what defense did the world have against the snakes' superior technology?

His stomach lurched and churned. What was the use of fighting and freeing the world if the weapons man created would eventually destroy the planet? Sheryl Lee had to be wrong about the effects of the red dust. She had to be!

Once again Rick surveyed the arid plain they were

walking on. Was this the future that awaited the rest of the world? Would the green forests and prairies slowly die, killed by a bacteria developed to slay an enemy not born of this planet?

No! Rick refused to accept that vision of the future. Even if the red dust caused the mutations Sheryl Lee detailed, there had to be a way to reverse its deadly effects. Those who had developed the toxin could destroy it—after the Visitors were driven from the world once again.

"Surfer Boy." Sheryl Lee nudged his shoulder. "I think we underestimated the distance we traveled before *Wanda Sue* was shot down."

"Huh?" Rick looked up, coming out of his dark reflections. "Damn!"

Ahead of them the ground abruptly opened. A canyon dropping at least eight hundred feet to its floor stretched for a mile before them.

"How?" Rick doubted his eyes. "This wasn't here a minute ago. How could it just appear?"

Sheryl Lee's mouth gave a funny little twist, and she shrugged. "It's the country's flatness. It hides even the smallest depression in the land. Whole armies of Comanche Indians used to hide from their pursuers in gullies. They weren't detected until it was too late."

Rick half listened to the redhead's history of this portion of Texas. In truth, he didn't give a damn about Comanches or how they used the land. The question was how were they going to cross this ragged trench that wind and water had cut into the earth?

Stepping to the edge of the canyon, he peered down and realized that the answer to his unspoken question was that they weren't!

A sheer face of limestone dropped four hundred feet below him before disappearing into a steep slope of sand and talus that fell to the canyon floor. Without mountain-climbing gear, or at least a stout rope, there was no way to make it down that first four hundred feet.

"This is the edge of the Caprock, isn't it?" he asked, looking east, then west. The canyon sliced through the land for as far as he could see in both directions.

"No." Sheryl Lee's head moved from side to side. "This is just one of several canyons that cut into the Caprock."

While she described the difficulties pioneers had in acsending the escarpmentlike walls of the Caprock, Rick studied the canyon floor. It appeared no more hospitable than the sheer faces of the walls. Rugged ravines and hills covered in thickly growing mesquite were everywhere. Even if they could reach the floor, it would take hours to cross a mile of imposing terrain below.

"What do we do now?" He stepped from the canyon's edge and looked at the fiery-haired beauty.

Sheryl Lee didn't answer. Her gaze focused on a distant finger of dust that rose from the flatlands behind them.

"What is it?" Rick squinted, but couldn't make out anything.

"Don't know, Surfer Boy," Sheryl Lee said, her voice no more than a whisper. "But I reckon we're fixin' to find out. It's comin' this way."

Chapter 8

The canary's head tilted from side to side. Its tiny dark eyes homed in on the fingers that flipped the latch to the cage and eased the door wide. It chirped and hopped about on its perch until it faced the unbarricaded avenue to freedom.

Garth's slitted eyes, human-imitating contact lenses abandoned in the solitude of his own quarters, narrowed so that only a hint of the reptilian orange sparked behind his eyelids. His lips pursed, and he whistled a weak imitation of the small bird's song.

"It's the only chance you'll get," he crooned gently to the canary. "Fly from your cage and you're free. Remain and . . ."

The delicate bird ruffled yellow feathers and once again cocked its head from side to side, cautiously examining the open door. Garth's alien heart quickened. The canary was going to try for freedom!

The bird's wings fluttered. It launched itself toward the gaping opening. Across the large wire cage it darted, intent only on escape from the metal prison.

Like a scene viewed in super slow motion, Garth watched the colorful creature's flight. He saw the strain of its tiny wings as they carried the plump body toward the open door. He watched in wonderment while tail feathers shifted to accommodate the bird's trajectory. Each small movement was beauty itself, a poem to the majesty of nature. Garth's heart felt as though it might explode from his chest.

The canary's head, then wings, fluttered through the open door. Its angle of flight abruptly changed as the fragile bird swerved upward to seek the safety of height.

At that same instant Garth's mouth snapped open. His tongue, red and moist, flicked out, a miniature biological whip. It struck, wrapping itself around the bird, before the canary's tail cleared the door. Then it coiled back, bringing the struggling morsel of yellow into waiting jaws that chomped once.

Then Garth swallowed.

It remains. . . . The primitive hunting instinct remains as sharp and focused as always. Garth, as he had done countless times in his life, tried to imagine himself climbing from the prehistoric swamps of his home world when his distant ancestors had ruled. They had survived, and were he thrown into similar circumstances, so would he—of that he was certain!

Beneath the thin veneer of civilization, the hunter dwelled in the soul of his people. That and only that sparked and fanned their greatness. Those who denied the hunter were destined to be no more than slaves. Those who worshiped the hunter—not even the stars were a limit to them.

Garth sank into the cushions of his chair. The hunter ruled his soul. This little game he played with bird and rodent was a daily sacrifice he offered up to his bloody god, a prayer that he laid at the feet of the force that molded the race humans called the Visitors.

Usually after the small game a deep sense of satisfaction suffused every cell of his body. For a moment he could forget the constant demands placed on the shoulders of a Mother Ship commander. Today that calming relaxation was denied him.

Damn the red-haired human bitch! he thought, cursing the source of his unrest. For months he had mentally savored and relished the method by which he would make the female pay for the hand she had cost him. Now the woman had robbed him of that pleasure. He viewed her death as a personal slap in the face. It was as though she had walked into the beam of one of his shock troopers' rifles to spit in his eye one last time.

Damn! He slammed a balled fist into the arm of his chair. How he regretted leaving her body on that table back in Dallas. The least he could have done was to have brought the corpse with him and dined on it this night.

Garth's head moved from side to side. *There would have been only bitterness in such a meal. Besides, the bitch was probably stringy!*

The thought provided no comfort. With vengeance so close, victory had been snatched from his hand. And like it or not, nothing remained to quiet the fury that consumed his breast.

"Commander Garth," a female voice imposed itself on the silence of his quarters.

Garth glared at the intercom grille set into his desk. "I left specific orders not to be disturbed for an hour."

"My apologies, Commander, but your standing orders call for immediate notification of any missing ship."

Swallowing a string of curses that would have ended with a double-rank demotion for the woman on the other end of the intercom, Garth asked, "Missing ship? Where?"

"Lubbock sector," the grille hissed the answer. "Two-person skyfighter on routine reconnaissance out of the Abilene Processing Center is reported two hours overdue in its return to base."

"You call this immediate reporting?" Garth's fury grew.

Five skyfighters had been mysteriously shot down in that sector in the past two months. The only hint of the cause that had brought down those ships was the fragmented communiqué that reported one of the vessels had engaged a propeller-powered human aircraft in combat. The wreckage of each of the five ships had eventually been found—all riddled by large-caliber machine guns.

"Commander, the communiqué from Abilene just arrived, I assure you," the woman on the intercom replied.

"And their plans for search and rescue?"

"No plans were included in the message, Commander," the woman said. "Abilene reports that all its skyfighters are presently assigned as escorts for the squad-vehicle wing en route to the Mother Ship."

Garth swung about, fingers dancing over the keys of a computer terminal on his desk. The screen above the keyboard flickered. Flight plans for every craft in his command scrolled onto the monitor.

He cursed. As evening approached, the majority of his ships, skyfighters and squad vehicles were returning to the Houston Mother Ship with their precious food cargo—humans neatly packed away and sealed in their cold-storage capsules.

"Very well," Garth said when he returned to the intercom. "Transmit my orders to Abilene. I want a full search for the missing ship the moment the skyfighters return to the base. And this time I want some answers. Make certain they understand that heads will roll unless an explanation for the losses is presented to me. Six ships shot down in two months is far too many to tolerate!"

"Yes, sir. Your orders will be transmitted immediately." The intercom clicked off.

Garth sank back into his chair. The image of a dead woman stretched atop a table in Dallas pushed thoughts of the missing skyfighters from his mind.

Chapter 9

The finger of dust grew to a minor cloud that approached closer with each heartbeat. Rick and Sheryl Lee edged behind the tough, gnarled trunks of a clump of mesquite trees and squatted there. With eyes glued on the swirling dust, Uzi and liberated Visitor energy pistols ready, they waited.

The dark form heading the dust cloud slowly became the distinct silhouette of an open jeep with a lone man behind the wheel. The dust rose from a long bundle of mesquite branches dragging behind the vehicle as it bounced and rattled across the rocky flatlands.

Rick raised the Uzi, held it stiff-armed before him, and braced his right arm at the wrist with his left hand. He lined up the jeep's driver in the sight. His finger tightened around the trigger, ready to squeeze the moment the man was in range.

Sheryl Lee reached up and tugged his arms down. She gave him a stern scowl.

"He's alone. Let's at least give him a chance to talk before you fill him full of holes, Surfer Boy."

"He could be a Visitor in radio contact with his superiors." Rick jerked away from the redhead and lifted the Uzi once more.

"And he could be human!" Sheryl Lee wrenched his arms down a second time. "There's still people in this part of the country. He might be able to help us. Which is a hell of a lot more than you've managed to do." Her eyes darted to the canyon at their backs.

"We can't . . ." Rick started, then gulped.

The firm barrel of an energy pistol jammed into the young man's ribs.

"Don't try me," Sheryl Lee said before Rick could utter another word. "This country breeds some mighty tough old buzzards. Right now a live one could get our fat out of the fire. Understand?"

Rick nodded and lowered the Uzi. With Sheryl Lee's stolen gun nestled against his ribs, he watched the sand-colored jeep brake twenty feet from the mesquites. The driver rose so that a head topped by a red and white "gimme" cap poked over a dusty windshield.

"You two have covered more ground than two jackrabbits with coyotes on their tails," a man's voice, with the same thick drawl Joe Bob had possessed, called to them. "I didn't think I'd catch up with you before the lizards did. Come on out. You're among friends."

Sheryl Lee's pistol came away from Rick's side when she stood and stepped from the mesquites. The barrel immediately leaped up, and she held the lone man in her sights.

"I think it's you who better step out, friend," she said in that arctic voice Rick had heard once before. He preferred it when it was directed at someone else, especially now that he realized how deadly the redhead was with the pistol. "I'd also suggest you hold your hands above your head as you step out, friend."

"Right. I'm movin' nice and easy. I wouldn't want you to burn a hole through the man that's driven all day just to rescue such a pretty li'l' lady."

With hands stretched high, a man in his late fifties or early sixties stepped from the jeep and walked toward the mesquites. He halted when Sheryl Lee's pistol jerked nervously.

"Take the gun from our friend here, Surfer Boy."
Sheryl Lee gave her head a toss in Rick's direction.

Uzi leveled to spray a burst of angry lead, Rick
hastened to the man's side. Except for the gimme cap that
proclaimed Wayne Feeds on its front, the jeep's driver
might have stepped out of some grade-B western. He
wore a white western shirt complete with mother-of-pearl
snap buttons, faded jeans that were more gray than blue,
and round-toed cowboy boots scarred and scuffed from
years of hard wear. About his hip was holstered a
chrome-plated pistol. Rick grasped the gun's butt and
slipped it from a tooled-leather sheath.

"Handle that real gentle like, son," the man said with
a smile that deeply creased a narrow, sun-and-wind-
weathered face. "That hogleg's a bit of history. Used to
belong to my great-granddaddy Scoggin. A genuine Colt
forty-five Peacemaker. Haven't made them like that in
over a century."

The heavy revolver felt like the genuine article in
Rick's hand. Teflon-coated bullets were visible within the
weapon's cylinder. He showed them to Sheryl Lee as she
stepped closer with the energy pistol still aimed at the
stranger's chest.

"The only thing that seems to work these days when a
man goes snake huntin'," the man said when he noticed
what drew their interest. "Those and a good Mustang."

Rick's jaw sagged. "Mustang? You?"

"One and the same." The man's grin widened so that
it seemed to split his narrow face in two. Blue-gray eyes
sparkled with delight beneath tufts of salt-and-pepper
hair, which poked from under his cap. "Reckon I left in a
mite of a hurry this mornin'. Was running low on fuel or
I'd have tried to make a landin'. Thought you two would
have sense enough to stay by that belly-floundered C-47
until someone came along."

Sheryl Lee poked at his chest when he attempted to
lower his arms. "A few bullets and a mention of some

old fighter plane aren't enough to convince me you're real, friend. Surfer Boy, check the jeep for a radio."

"Name's Scoggin, Charlie Scoggin." The man's eyes followed Rick to the dusty jeep. "Couldn't we talk about this on the way back to my place? Ain't safe out here. Surprised the Visitors haven't come along 'fore now, lookin' for that skyfighter I brought down this mornin'."

"No radio," Rick called after a quick search of the jeep. "And I can't find any other weapons."

"We're really wastin' precious time, li'l' lady," Charlie Scoggin urged. "I didn't come all the way out here just to end up in some lizard's fryin' pan. I *can* talk while I drive."

"Whadya think?" Sheryl Lee asked when Rick returned to her side.

"He's unarmed, and he can drive," Rick mused aloud. "And like the man said, we run the risk of Visitors every minute we're in the open."

"Okay, Charlie Scoggin, back into the jeep." Sheryl Lee motioned him toward the vehicle with the pistol's barrel. "And please, no funny business. Surfer Boy here and I aren't in a very humorous mood."

With two pistols following his every move, the old man eased into the driver's seat and sat there with his hands on the wheel until Sheryl Lee and Rick climbed into the jeep. When the redhead nodded, he twisted the key in the ignition and brought the jeep to life with a tap of his foot on the gas pedal.

"I'd feel a mite better if ya'll point those things elsewheres." Scoggin eased the jeep into first gear and did a slow 180-degree turn to head it back in the direction it had come.

Neither of the muzzles drooped. Scoggin shrugged and turned his attention to the terrain.

"Why the shrubbery tied to the back of the jeep, old man?" Rick glanced at the mesquite branches trailing the vehicle.

"Haven't watched too many cowboy movies, have you, son?" Scoggin wrestled the brim of his cap close to his face and smiled. "If you had, you'd know it's an old trick the Comanches used to cover a trail. Visitors would spot my tires tracks from half a mile up if I didn't erase 'em as I went."

More Texas history. Rick groaned inwardly as he settled back for the ride. *First from Sheryl Lee and now from this old man. Is that all Texans can talk about?*

"Now, friend," Sheryl Lee said, "why don't you tell us about yourself?"

Charlie Scoggin needed no further encouragement. For the next hour he related a full family history, including an account of his great-grandfather's career as a West Texas sheriff in the late 1800s. He then gave a thumbnail sketch of his grandfather's and father's lives as ranchers and the discovery of oil on the family land after World War II.

"Which wasn't as important to me as what broke out halfway around the world in a place called Korea," Charlie Scoggin said. "I joined up and found myself in pilot trainin'."

He explained that he was shipped overseas with the Eighteenth Fighter-Bomber Group. "The Eighth, Thirty-fifth, and Forty-eighth all flew Mustangs durin' the early days of the war. However, the Eighteenth stuck with P-51s until January 1953. There's no denyin' the excitement of takin' the joystick of a jet, but it didn't compare to a Mustang. That baby got into my blood and never left."

When Charlie's air force career ended, he entered commercial aviation, flying passenger liners and moving on to the big jets. "West Texas and raisin' cattle just weren't excitin' enough to compete with the skies."

He met his wife, Thelma, on a flight from Atlanta to Houston. "We had us two fine boys. Both live up north with their own families now—thank the Lord. Didn't like it when they left Texas, but it's worked out for the best."

"Where's Thelma now?" This from Sheryl Lee.

Charlie swallowed and tears misted his eyes as they glanced at the reds and oranges that streaked the western sky in a magnificent sunset. "She died in Houston. It was durin' the Visitors' first attempt to take over."

Thelma was undergoing minor surgery in a Houston hospital when the Visitors temporarily cut electrical power to the Gulf city as a display of their power. The hospital had emergency generators, Scoggin said, but by the time they were cut in, it was too late to save his wife.

"It was then that I joined the resistance," he said. "After the Visitors were driven away, I left our home and Houston and returned to the family ranch."

Sheryl Lee's energy pistol lowered as the sun sank below the horizon. Neither she nor Rick asked any further questions while Charlie maneuvered the jeep south through the dusk that covered the plains.

"About ten minutes more." Charlie glanced at his two companions. "We've got to cut onto the highway to get down the Caprock. Usually stay clear of paved roads. Visitors keep an eye peeled on them."

Driving lightless through the night, the Korean War veteran wheeled the jeep onto a wide ribbon of asphalt highway. Rick felt the older man's foot nudge the accelerator closer to the floor. The highway dropped abruptly in a sharp angle of decline. Even in the light of a waning moon, Rick could see the rugged rock formations highway engineers had cut through to lay their road up to the Caprock.

When the road leveled, Charlie turned north and drove along the base of the escarpment for a couple of miles before maneuvering the jeep into a canyon that sliced westward into the Caprock. "Home, sweet home."

Rick peered into the murky night ahead. If a house or

even a shack stood within the canyon, he missed it. All
he saw were canyon walls, rock, sand, and cedars and
mesquite growing to each side near the talus that spilled
from the Caprock.

"Sand's light here, covering solid rock," Charlie said.
"Makes for a natural runway. The canyon also provides
the perfect cover. Unless you know what you're lookin'
for, it's impossible to spot my place from the air."

From the ground too. Rick still couldn't see any sign
of a house or other indication that man had ever been
within the canyon.

"Thelma and I built us a getaway here during the early
seventies. With all the hoorah about ecology, it seemed
to make sense that the place should blend into the
country as much as possible." Charlie drove around a
rise of sand and rock that pushed from the ground at the
end of the canyon. "We decided on one of them
underground homes. Didn't take but a few dollars more
to make my hangar part of a matching pair. Rock and
sand are cheap in this country."

Rick whistled softly. The west side of the false mound
revealed a door and a wide picture window in an
underground dwelling that faced the western wall of the
canyon. Beside the house, much in the manner most
homes have attached garages, was an open single-plane
hangar containing the Mustang the Californian had first
seen fending off the skyfighter that had brought *Wanda
Sue* to the ground.

Charlie wheeled into the hangar's darkness and halted
beside the P-51's wing tip. He slid from the jeep and
motioned to a door on his left.

"House is through there. I keep the curtains drawn up
front, so you can switch on the lights. You'll find coffee
on the stove. Go on in and make yourselves comfortable.
I'll be along in a minute or five. Got to close up for the
night."

Sheryl Lee accepted the old man's invitation, but Rick

sat in the jeep staring up at the Mustang's shadowy form. Inside, Sheryl Lee switched on the lights. A soft yellow glow intruded into the darkness, highlighting the old fighter's naked metal body. Even on the ground the plane looked like a shark of the air.

"She's a beauty, ain't she?" Charlie grinned as he walked to a switch on the wall near the entrance of the hangar. He pushed an oversized black button and the building's door rolled noisily down from the ceiling. "She's a damn sight fancier than the one I flew in Korea. Called a Cavalier Mustang III. After the war a Florida company modified a lot of the surplus Mustangs for military use in Central and South America. Got a Rolls-Royce turboprop engine capable of four hundred seventy knots dash speed. Those are six fifty-caliber machine guns in her wings, son."

When the hangar door closed, Charlie switched on the lights, revealing the fighter in its full splendor. Rick noticed that five carefully drawn red squares had been painted on the aircraft's fuselage just in front of its elongated canopy. At the center of each square was a black ⌐•¦⌐ —the emblem under which the Visitors

came to dominate Earth.

"Have to paint another one of those on her before I go up again," Charlie said with a chuckle. "Like to see every damn inch of her painted like that before we make our last flight together."

"Six kills," Rick said without trying to disguise his admiration. "If this were standard battle, that would make you an ace plus one."

"Ain't no war *standard*, son. And *ace* don't mean a hill of beans, especially to me." Charlie's gaze ran lovingly over the gleaming hull of the fighter. "Bought her as surplus in Mexico in 'sixty-five. Always intended to donate her to the Confederate Air Force, but once I got her back into shape, I couldn't bear to part with her. Raced her a bit when I had the time."

Rick listened to the old man talk, remembering an article he had read about the Confederate Air Force. The group of Texas businessmen and sportsmen restored and maintained World War II war-birds and kept their prizes at an airport in far South Texas. For a moment, he visualized a fighter wing composed of men the caliber of Charlie Scoggin.

It was an impossible daydream, Rick realized. The Visitors were firmly entrenched in South Texas. If the lizards had heard of the flying museum, he was certain they had destroyed it.

"What about the machine guns?" Rick asked as he stepped from the jeep and stretched. "I'm certain the government frowned on that part of the restoration."

"I was always of the opinion that what Uncle Sugar didn't know about didn't hurt him." Charlie chuckled as he walked back toward the jeep. "After we first drove off the Visitors, I made a flight down to Mexico City. Only took a couple of days to locate six operational machine guns and the ammo to go with them. Don't know why I felt like I needed them, though. Guess I just didn't want to get caught with my pants draggin' around my ankles again."

Charlie's feeling was shared by a majority of Americans, Rick realized. After the red dust sent the Visitors back into space, purchasing rifles and pistols had become a national pastime.

"I smell coffee." Charlie motioned him toward the door. "No need wastin' any more time out here."

Together they entered a house that was compact and surprisingly modern in its design. Where Rick expected to find antiques, he saw chrome, glass, and plastic. If the home's interior and the fighter that sat in the hangar were an indication of their owner, Charlie Scoggin, with his

West Texas drawl and good-ol'-boy manner, disguised a man of hidden complexities.

They found Sheryl Lee seated at a circular kitchen table, nursing a mug of coffee. Two more mugs sat steaming on the table. Rick sank into a chair on her right and sipped from a mug. The coffee, strong and hot, rolled down his throat and into a welcoming stomach.

"Unless you two managed to catch yourselves an armadillo and ate shell and all, I didn't catch a sign of you having eaten today," Charlie said as he tugged open a refrigerator door. "Ain't got a thing to offer you, except maybe some steak and eggs. I live pretty simple."

"Steak and eggs. I'd kill for steak and eggs right now."

Rick grinned. He could almost hear Sheryl Lee's mouth watering as she spoke. He knew he felt his own mouth watering.

"Need some help?" Sheryl Lee started to rise, but Charlie waved her back to her seat.

"Ya'll just sit and rest. Won't take but a few minutes to whip this up. How you like your beefsteak cooked?" Charlie lifted three slabs of deep-red meat from the refrigerator.

"Rare," Rick piped up, and received the sort of stares from his two companions that were normally reserved for transgressors of society's most rigid taboos.

Fifteen minutes later he understood why. While he gratefully savored a thick, juicy steak smothered in four eggs, Sheryl Lee and Charlie gnawed contentedly at steaks that had been so overcooked the meat looked dry and gray.

"Must raise 'em different in California." Charlie shook his head as he watched Rick cut another bite from his meal. "Don't know why your momma even bothered cookin' for you, son. Hell, been easier to turn you loose to run alongside the steer and just let you take a bite anytime you got hungry."

"It is a mite bloody, Surfer Boy." Sherly Lee's nose wrinkled in disgust. "You're in Texas now. Ought to learn to eat meat in a civilized manner. It would make it easier on the rest of us."

Rick ignored the gibes, sliced another bite of the red meat, and popped it into his mouth. "And you two might as well be eating charcoal."

Neither answered, only shook their heads again as though to say that there were some people beyond help. Rick smiled and hungrily cut into the steak again, topped it with egg yellow, and stuffed it into his mouth.

"You've let me pretty well talk myself out about myself." Charlie washed down a mouthful with a swig of coffee. "But you haven't told me a thing about yourselves or what you were doing in that old C-47."

"Smuggling medical supplies into Dallas and Fort Worth," Sheryl Lee answered between bites.

She quickly recounted the flight to Los Angeles, how she and Joe Bob had broken into a medical warehouse, and their chance meeting with Rick. Charlie listened without interrupting, only nodding and mming occasionally.

"Once we were in the air, everything was going fine until we ran into that skyfighter," she said. "After that, you know what happened."

"Seems to me," Charlie paused to drain the last of his coffee, "that ya'll've done most of the hard work bringin' them supplies this far. Ought to be some way of gettin' them the rest of the way into Fort Worth, if not Dallas."

"Ought to be." Sherly Lee pushed back from the table. An empty plate glistened before her. "But I haven't come up with any ideas yet."

"If something ain't done soon, it'll be too late," Charlie mused aloud as he leaned back in his chair and stared at the ceiling. "Visitors'll be lookin' for that skyfighter. When they find it, they'll find your medical supplies too."

Neither Rick nor Sheryl Lee answered. Charlie shoved himself away from the table and stood.

"Seems to me it would be a sin to let the snakes get their hands on those supplies after you've hauled 'em so far, li'l' lady." Charlie waved an arm to the interior of the house. "Ya'll make yourselves comfortable. There's a drop or two of bourbon in that cabinet. And beds if you want to catch up on a little shut-eye."

Charlie started toward the door leading to the hangar when Sheryl Lee called to him. "Charlie, what's the matter? Where you goin'?"

"To check on a couple of things," he answered. "Don't want to get your hopes up, but I got me half an idea about how we might just be able to get those supplies of yours."

"How?"

"Give me an hour or three," he replied. "If it works, then we're in business. If not, then we're no worse off than we are now."

With that, he opened the door and stepped into the hangar. Outside, Rick heard the massive door rumbling open. Moments later the jeep started, purred for a few seconds, then trundled away into the night.

Rick looked at Sheryl Lee with eyebrows raised in question. He received a shrug in answer. For a moment they just sat there, neither speaking nor moving. Sheryl Lee finally broke the silence.

"Think I'll take the old man at his word and make myself comfortable." She looked around. "There's bound to be a bathroom somewhere, and a nice hot shower sounds like a bit of heaven right now."

As she rose, Rick pushed from the table and motioned to the liquor cabinet. "Want a drink waiting when you get out?"

"Surfer Boy, I can't think of a nicer touch. About two

fingers of bourbon—no water or ice." She smiled and strode off in search of the bath.

Rick turned his attention to the liquor cabinet and found half a bottle of bourbon and two glasses. He poured a couple of healthy shots into each glass and diluted his with an equal amount of water. With drinks in hand, he wandered from the kitchen into the living room. Placing Sheryl Lee's bourbon on a glass table, he sank into the cushions of a sofa and inhaled half his own drink.

Somewhere behind him, he heard the sound of running water. He smiled; Sheryl Lee had found her shower. Taking another sip, he closed his eyes and imagined the water was a gentle spring rain, although he suspected cooling rains were a rarity in this dry, rugged country.

Caprocks, mesquites, Texas! He let another sip of the bourbon and water trickle soothingly down his throat. So much had happened, so much had changed. It was hard to believe that less than twenty-four hours ago he had followed Mike Donovan through a rent in the fence surrounding John Wayne International Airport.

"You're not fallin' asleep on me, are you?"

Rick opened his eyes and turned. Sheryl Lee walked into the living room wrapped in a white terry-cloth robe that was obviously Charlie Scoggin's size. She crossed to the sofa, lifted her drink, and plopped down beside Rick.

"Feel like a new woman." She grinned, tipped her glass to him, then drained the drink in a single swallow that ended with a pleased sigh.

Rick contained a chuckle that tried to push from his throat. Sheryl Lee Darcy constantly amazed him. The khaki-clad angel who had doctored his leg wound was gone. Now in her place was a radiant woman. He inhaled, the clean aroma of soap coyly taunting his nostrils.

"I'm not sayin' you turned ripe or anything out in the sun today, Surfer Boy, but you might consider a little soap and water yourself," she said as she leaned her head against the back of the sofa and closed her eyes. "You need to be careful with that leg. Keep it clean so it doesn't get infected."

"I might take you up on that if I can convince my body it can still move." He drained the rest of his drink and placed the empty glass on the table.

"How's the leg? Still hurt?" She spoke without opening her eyes.

"Pain's gone. Walked it out, I think." He flexed his right leg. "Still a bit stiff, especially when I let it rest. But I think your earlier diagnosis was correct. I'll live."

He smiled and turned to the young redhead just in time to see her head slowly roll to the right until it came to rest against his shoulder. Throaty purring sounds accompanied the nestling nudges of her head, then there was only the steady, deep rhythmic breathing of sleep.

Careful not to disturb her, Rick lifted his arm and wrapped it about her shoulder, protectively drawing her to his side. The warmth of her body suffused the layers of fabric separating them. He closed his eyes, a smile playing on his lips. It was a feeling he could easily grow accustomed to.

Chapter 10

Commander Garth of the Houston Mother Ship stood in the K deck control room. Beyond the chamber's sweeping windows squad vehicles entered and exited the ship in a steady stream. Garth silently nodded his approval of the scene. A sense of pride filled his chest. The same scene was presently being repeated on every flight deck in the gargantuan vessel.

Outside, fatigue crews scurried to each landing vessel and swung open its side hatch. Immediately, portable conveyer belts were dollied into position. One by one translucent capsules emptied from the belly of each ship. The process would continue throughout the night as the Mother Ship accepted the daily harvest from Texas' processing centers.

Garth turned from the panoramic view of the flight deck and strolled to the rear of the control room to step into a waiting elevator. There his voice command closed the door and sent the lift shooting up ten levels, where it halted abruptly, and the door hissed open again.

Stepping out, Garth's gaze was met by the same sort of industrious activity he had seen below. Here, within one of the ship's massive storage rooms, fatigue crews took the capsules fed to them from the flight-deck conveyer system and neatly packed the precious cargo away.

"Commander." A young lieutenant glanced up from a control console and snapped to attention. "I didn't hear the elevator, sir."

Garth smiled and nodded. "As you were."

The lieutenant's eyes shifted back to the control console. His fingers danced over a keypad, and a mini-display screen winked alive with a line of phosphorescent green figures. A pleased smile moved over his human-imitating lips.

"We're above our quota for this week, Commander Garth," he reported. "If all continues at this rate, we should reach a new high in processing. At least two hundred thousand, I would estimate."

"Fine, Lieutenant, fine. Twenty-five percent above production when Mary was supervising processing. Our Great Leader will be pleased." Garth granted the lieutenant a smile as he walked to the railed edge of the concourse on which he stood.

Mary, who had earned the name of Dark Death of Dallas while commanding the Dallas–Fort Worth processing centers, had been one of Scientific Commander Diana's personal students. The woman, along with several other high-ranking fleet officers, had died when resistance fighters had bombed a party given by Diana in the California town of Playa.

Garth did not mourn the loss. For all her flash and show, Mary had been no more than one of Diana's spies, reporting his every move to her mentor. That processing had so dramatically increased since the woman's demise would be a sharp thorn in Diana's side.

With hands firmly planted on the rail, Garth stared across a gaping canyon that yawned on each side of the concourse. His gaze moved over a glistening wall of gelatin-filled capsules. Slowly his neck craned back. For as far as he could see above him, the wall of capsules lofted upward, disappearing in the chamber's own misty atmosphere. The same scene repeated itself in reverse when he looked down.

From top to bottom of the great Mother Ship, this artificial canyon stretched, over three human miles, with a width and length each equal to a mile. Gradually, methodically, this chamber and its sisters on the ship would be filled with the capsules the squad vehicles brought each day. Just contemplating the millions upon millions of capsules required to complete the task left him dizzy.

And in each capsule—a human, quick frozen in suspended animation. Each awaited the time they would be reawakened. Some would be given the honor of taking to the battlefield and giving their lives for the glory of the Great Leader in his never-ending battle against the "Others," that malignant race who opposed the Visitors' right to rule the stars. Far more would find their way onto reptilian tables.

Garth pivoted on the balls of his feet and started back to the elevator. Once again he saw the lieutenant busily punching a capsule count into the Mother Ship's computer. The scrolling minidisplay tickled something at the back of Garth's mind.

With that elusive something flitting about in his head, Garth entered the elevator and barked a command for it to return to his quarters. The mechanism responded by beginning its long ascent to the Mother Ship's uppermost levels.

The computer. Garth gave a name to the thought that evaded him. The ship's computer might provide an avenue to vent the frustration and anger gnawing at him. The computer held personal records on every resistance member his intelligence network had been able to identify. All he had to do was pull the records on the redheaded bitch who had died before he had gotten to her.

Yes, he nodded to himself. Something hidden in those records would give him a key, provide a method to finally repay the female for all that she had cost him.

When the elevator stopped and its door opened, Garth strode straight for his desk to punch in the name that had haunted him all day. Seconds later the computer flashed the information he sought on the monitor. It took no more than a cursory perusal of the electronic records to locate the key he desired.

Chapter 11

A distant rumble of thunder intruded into a gentle dream of a sunny, warm southern California afternoon. Rick tried to block out the disquieting sound, but it only mounted until the comforting images that caressed him shattered.

He opened his eyes and blinked. Momentary disorientation gave way to the realization that he still sat in the living room of Charlie Scoggin's underground home. Sheryl Lee, nestled in the hollow of his shoulder, stirred, her emerald-green eyes languidly opening. A sleepy smile slid across her red lips.

"And I was worried about you fallin' asleep on *me*." She lazily lifted her head, sat up, and stretched. "I could use about forty-eight more hours of that."

Rick only half listened to her. He concentrated on the thunderlike rumble that had destroyed the dream and awakened him. In spite of the fact that he was now awake, the thunder continued.

"What is it?" Sheryl Lee's brow furrowed.

"Listen. It's growing louder."

She did, her head cocking to the right. "It sounds like a car."

"Or cars." Rick shoved himself up from the sofa and hastened into the kitchen, where he snatched the Uzi from atop the table.

"Surfer Boy?"

"I think you'd better dress. It sounds like we've got

company coming," he replied, turning back to the robe-clad woman.

Sheryl Lee didn't question him, but darted into the house's interior.

Tucking his stolen energy pistol into the belt of his jeans, Rick moved to the door leading to the hangar and opened it. The sound was louder—the mounting rumble of several approaching motors.

"Son of a bitch!" The curse hissed through the young man's clenched teeth.

With his folksy ways and steak and eggs, they had allowed Charlie Scoggin to garner their trust. Then they had let the old man leave to summon the snakes!

No. Rick refused to accept the scenario his panicked brain pieced together. He had seen Charlie and his Mustang in action. The man was no collaborator. Of that Rick was certain.

Then what?

He opened the door wider and started to step out. A hand grasped his shoulder from behind. Before he could spin about, Sheryl Lee spoke.

"You're not leavin' without me, Surfer Boy. We've come this far together; it's no time to break up a partnership."

"I was just going to slip outside to see if—"

"Then we'll slip out together," she cut the explanation and nodded for him to lead the way.

Outside they moved around the perimeter of the mound of sand and rock covering Scoggin's underground home and disguised hangar. In the light of the waning moon, they saw Charlie's jeep at the head of a caravan of seven pickup trucks that rolled over the canyon floor.

"What in hell?" Rick used the words to conceal his sigh of relief.

Sheryl Lee only shook her head in mute answer as they watched the jeep swing around the mounded sand.

Charlie, a broad grin stretching from one ear to the other, waved them to follow him when he passed.

"What is this?" Sheryl Lee trotted to the man as he halted and slid from the driver's seat.

"The way to save them medical supplies, li'l' lady. That's if the lizards haven't already gotten at 'em," Charlie said when Rick joined his companions. The older man turned to the pickups that rounded the mound. "Ain't as fast as airmail, but overland freight beats nothin' at all."

One by one the pickups halted. Cab doors swung wide and two men stepped from each of the vehicles. No, Rick corrected his first impression. Men and women with faces set like granite walked to where they stood.

"Folks," Charlie said, turning to the trucks' occupants, "I want you to meet the two brave young people I told you about—Sheryl Lee Darcy and Rick Hurley."

Smiles turned the stolid masks into warm human faces. Several arms shot out and hands grasped Sheryl Lee's and Rick's hands, shaking them.

"You two done yourself proud," a man spoke, while a woman said, "You kinda remind me of my own daughter. She was a student at Texas Tech when the Visitors hit Lubbock."

Charlie raised his arms and voice. "Folks, I know ya'll would like to visit and get to know these two, but time's one thing we're runnin' out of. If we're goin' to save the medical supplies, we've got to move—and move now."

"Then why're you wastin' time talkin', Charlie Scoggin?" a woman called out. "Let's get a move on."

"You heard the lady—move out." Charlie motioned Sheryl Lee and Rick into his jeep. "I'll explain everything as we go."

"What about weapons for these people?" Rick climbed into the rear of the jeep. "We might run into shock troopers out there."

"They've got shotguns and deer rifles in their pickups." Charlie eased beneath the steering wheel and turned the ignition key. He pumped the gas pedal two times when the motor caught, then shifted into gear. "I also told 'em to go for the head and legs, if it comes down to a fight. None of 'em have Teflon-coated bullets."

Rick glanced back as the truck convoy circled Scoggin's home and pulled onto the canyon floor. He could make out the vague forms of rifles racked in the rear windows of the pickups. While ordinary ammunition wouldn't penetrate the armor Visitor shock troopers wore over their chests and backs, shotguns and deer rifles would be deadly if aimed at heads and legs.

"Who are they?" Sheryl Lee asked.

"People, just people," Charlie replied.

Rick heard the names Charlie rattled off, but he couldn't retain them. They were farmers and ranchers, people the Korean War veteran merely described as "neighbors." Like the nameless woman who had compared Sheryl Lee to her daughter who had been caught in Lubbock during the Visitors' raids, all had family or friends who had died or disappeared when the snakes had returned to Earth.

"I don't think I'll be able to thank them enough, Charlie." Sheryl Lee glanced over her shoulder at the caravan of pickups that followed the jeep.

"You two are the ones they want to thank, honey." Charlie's expression was somber. "We're isolated out here, but every one of us knows what's going on. These folks aren't lucky like yours truly. I've got my Mustang; I can strike out. It's not much, I admit, but I can fight. My friends back there haven't had that chance."

He paused as though trying to find the right words. "You and your medical supplies have given them the chance they've been achin' for, li'l' lady. This is real, not just squad vehicles and skyfighters whining overhead beyond their reach. They've got something solid they can sink their teeth into. And believe me, once they take hold, they're like snappin' turtles; they won't let go no matter what!''

That familiar sensation Rick had felt on every one of his resistance missions filled his chest. How could anyone help but feel pride stirring? The men and women in the pickups were total strangers, yet they were laying their lives on the line this night to help those in distant Dallas and Fort Worth. He couldn't remember a single name Charlie had mentioned, but in that moment he loved each and every one of them and felt no shame in that love.

With the pickups lagging a mile behind, Charlie trundled the jeep cautiously toward the two abandoned wrecks that lay half buried in the sand.

"Looks clear." Charlie halted the jeep and pulled himself up so that he peered over the windshield.

"The lizards might have found the wreck and left shock troopers inside just in case we returned." Rick surveyed the C-47's wreckage. Nothing moved around it or the cracked hull of the skyfighter.

"Then we have a little surprise waitin' for them. Take a look into the toolbox to your right, son," Charlie directed.

Rick did and pulled out two bundles, each made up of four sticks of dynamite tied together with baling wire. A short fuse protruded from each bundle. "Where did you get these?"

"Emmett Voss had it at his place to help stubborn mesquite stumps out of the ground." Charlie handed Rick a lit cigar when he turned to face the Californian. "Keep that stogie burnin' cherry red. At the first sign of trouble, touch off one of those fuses and chuck the dynamite fast. You've got five-second fuses on both them bundles."

Placing one of the bundles carefully beside him, Rick accepted the cigar while maintaining a cautious distance between it and the bundle still in his right hand. He puffed at the cigar and did his best to stifle the nonsmoker's cough that lodged in his throat.

Chuckling, Charlie eased the jeep into gear once again and moved forward. "Now we'll see if snakes come out in the dark."

The fighter pilot's foot gently pressed the accelerator, the jeep inched toward the two wrecks. Sheryl Lee lifted her energy pistol and swung it from *Wanda Sue* to the skyfighter, ready for an attack from either of the downed aircraft.

Rick completely forgot the rancid taste of the cigar as his attention focused on the scene ahead. His eyes searched both C-47 and skyfighter, then probed the shadows cast by the dim moonlight. Nothing.

"So far, so good." Charlie halted twenty feet from *Wanda Sue*'s open hatch. He tugged the jeep's stick shift into neutral. "Sheryl Lee, slide over here while I check inside." He looked back at Rick. "You just stand by with that dynamite."

Before either could answer, Charlie stepped from the jeep and unholstered the ancient Peacemaker hung on his hip. Two metallic clicks sounded as he thumbed back the six-shooter's hammer and trotted to the transport plane's door. Back pressed against fuselage, he paused, listened for a few moments, then ducked inside. Five heartbeats later he emerged and held up a hand with rounded fore-finger and thumb touching to signal that everything was all right.

Still without a word, he darted to the skyfighter. Hesitating beside the rent in its side, he listened once again before entering. When he exited, he called out, "Rick, stow that dynamite and put out the cigar. There's a flashlight in the toolbox. Signal the others with two long beams."

Flipping the cigar away, the young freedom fighter exchanged the bundles of dynamite for the flashlight. He turned around, lifted the light, and flashed it for two seconds. He turned it off, then gave another flash. A pair of headlight beams blinked on and off twice in answer.

"We can have some of the boxes unloaded by the time the others get here." Sheryl Lee switched off the jeep's ignition and slipped from behind the wheel.

Replacing the flashlight, Rick climbed from the jeep and followed the redhead into *Wanda Sue*'s belly.

"That's the last one." Rick handed a box marked Bandages to a rancher named Jess Tubbs, then watched it proceed down the line of men and women to the waiting pickup.

"Took two hours." Charlie snapped the cover of a pocket watch closed and stuffed the timepiece into the coin pocket of his jeans. "I was hopin' we'd do it in half the time. But it's done and that's what counts. Soon as that tarp's tied down, we can get out of here."

"And leave Joe Bob?" Sheryl Lee glanced at Joe Bob's body, which still lay slumped in the pilot's seat where he had died.

Charlie drew a deep breath and released it in a slow hiss. "Some things don't sit right with a man, Sheryl Lee. Leavin' your friend there without a Christian burial is one of them. But I don't see any way round it. Leavin' him there like that just might convince the snakes that he was all alone in this plane. And that might give us the edge we need. Keep the Visitors off our tails for a while."

Sheryl Lee bit at her lower lip and looked back at the cockpit again. Hesitantly, she nodded. "He'd have probably wanted something like this anyway. The crazy bastard loved this old plane. No place else he'd rather be."

"Charlie," the lanky cattleman named Emmett Voss

called from outside the plane. "Everybody's loaded and lashed down."

"Then ya'll know what to do," Charlie answered when he and his young companions ducked out of the plane. "Meet us at the mouth of the canyon tomorrow an hour after sundown."

The farmers and ranchers turned and walked toward their trucks.

"Tomorrow?" This from Rick. "We're not leaving until tomorrow night?"

"This night's 'bout used up, son." Charlie pushed back his cap and stared at the starry sky. "We couldn't make more than thirty or forty miles 'fore sunup. There ain't much cover for at least a hundred miles. I don't want us to get caught sittin' out in the open. Tonight we all head home and get what rest we can, 'cause we'll be getting damned little of it come tomorrow night."

Truck engines started, and Rick turned to watch the seven pickups pull away, moving across the flatlands without the aid of their headlights.

"Help me tote that snake who nearly got you today back into the skyfighter, then we can be on our way," Charlie said.

Rick nodded and walked with the man to where the Visitor Sheryl Lee had killed earlier lay in the sand. With Charlie lifting the arms and Rick handling the legs, they carried the alien back into the skyfighter and placed him in the pilot's seat.

Charlie sucked at his teeth. "Wish to hell they were both burnt a little more. All it takes is a glance to see how both of 'em died."

Rick admitted the energy blast burns on both bodies were obvious. He pulled the Visitor pistol from his belt. "You want to do it . . . or shall I?"

"It's your gun, son." Charlie turned and walked from the ship as Rick lifted the gun and began to burn the bodies beyond recognition.

Two minutes later, when he exited the skyfighter, both aliens appeared to have died when their ship crashed and burned.

"Get me the hell out of here," was all the Californian said when he rejoined his companions in the jeep.

While Charlie steered over the night-shrouded plain, Rick leaned over the side of the jeep and heaved what remained of his supper. He had been wrong earlier when he accused the Visitors of robbing him of his humanity. What he had done back in the skyfighter had been dirty. And no matter how necessary his actions had been, he could not stop the nausea that painfully knotted his gut.

Chapter 12

Garth rubbed his right temple as he scanned the report on the missing skyfighter. Like the other five that had been shot down in the Lubbock sector, the craft was riddled with holes from a high-caliber machine gun.

"Whatever primitive weapon these humans, or human, are using, Yvonne, it is highly effective." He sank into his chair and stared at his science officer, who stood before his desk.

"The weapon was a machine gun of approximately fifty caliber," Yvonne replied. "However, it was not directly responsible for either the pilot's or co-pilot's death."

She pulled a folder from beneath her arm and passed it across the desk. "Here's the preliminary report from the medical staff. It basically says the co-pilot died from head injuries sustained in the crash, despite the burns covering fifty percent of his body."

"And the pilot?" Garth opened the folder and glanced at it.

"The burns were responsible for his death." Yvonne snorted, a sound that was closer to a hiss. "However, the injuries weren't caused by the skyfighter burning."

"Get to the point. I haven't time for playing games." Garth scooted to the edge of his chair and rested his arms on the desk.

"The point is that the pilot was killed and burned with one of our pistols. The co-pilot's corpse was burned by similar blasts. It was an attempt to make it appear that both deaths resulted from the crash," she answered. "My guess is that their own weapons were used."

"Their own weapons?" Garth's gaze returned to the crash report. He found a paragraph he had overlooked. Both the pilot's and co-pilot's side arms were missing from their holsters. "It seems that someone left out a small detail of their charade."

"If I may make another educated guess, I would speculate that the pilot of the human aircraft was not alone in the plane."

"Hmm." Garth noted that the shock troopers who discovered the wreckage found no signs of human activity about either the airplane or the skyfighter "Any specific reason for this conjecture?"

"This." Yvonne bent down, lifted a leather bag from the floor, and placed it on the desk.

"A woman's purse?" Garth hefted the bag and eyed it.

"The shock troopers found this stuffed beneath the co-pilot's seat on the downed plane," Yvonne explained. "I think it's easy to put one and one together and come up with the answer. The human co-pilot was a female who survived the crash, entered the skyfighter, and killed our two men. She then escaped on foot. Tracks are easy enough to erase in sand. It would have taken little effort on her part."

Garth nodded while he upended the purse and dumped its contents on the desk. "Pens, pencils, a comb, brush, and cosmetics—all normal for a human female. But nothing with which we might identify your human co-pilot."

"There's this." Yvonne dug into a pocket of her white lab smock and pulled out a black wallet. "This was found in the purse."

Garth arched an eyebrow when he accepted the billfold, but made no comment. He could allow Yvonne her dramatics as long as she continued to produce results.

Opening the wallet, Garth thumbed through an assortment of credit cards and photographs. His pulse doubled! Staring at him from out of a thin plastic envelope was the human bitch who had cost him his left hand!

Fingers trembling, he slowly went through the remaining photographs. A pleased smile twisted his lips. There on a driver's license issued by the Texas Highway Department he found the answer he sought—not only a name, but a color photograph! The family resemblance was incredible.

"I want this photograph enlarged and distributed to every pilot who flies over the sectors between Dallas and Lubbock." He slipped the license from the wallet and handed it to Yvonne. "Most of all I want this woman, this Sheryl Lee Darcy. If your theory is correct, she's alone and on foot. See that she is found and brought here, Yvonne."

"Yes, Commander." The Houston Mother Ship's science officer pivoted and strode from Garth's office.

So the bitch's offspring still lives! Garth felt the hunter stir within his breast. *And soon she shall bear the child I had planned for her mother!*

Chapter 13

Lightning walked across the sky. Twisted legs of living fire, actinic arcs danced on the southern horizon. As though in chain reaction, new bolts shot northward, giving birth in turn to another wave of sizzling energy until the unbridled electricity disappeared on the northern horizon.

A grinding rumble, like the sound of mountains colliding in midair, barely reached Rick Hurley's ears before another barrage of spidery bolts lit the sky.

"Damn!" Charlie Scoggin tugged the collar of his shirt high around his neck as a moist gush of wind ripped across the plain. "We're in for a frog strangler. No more'n half an hour away."

Thunder rolled and the sky went blue-white, lightning illuminating a churning front of clouds that approached from the southeast. Rick squinted in an attempt to find the tops of the massive monsters. He couldn't.

The fiery display provided just enough light to ignite his imagination. The thunderheads that filled his mind's eye loomed upward to the very boundary of heaven itself. Another gush of wind sent a shudder quaking through the jeep. He shivered with the realization that his imagination might not be that far off target.

"Son of a bitch!" Charlie cursed again. He shook his head when another series of lightning bolts raced from horizon to horizon. "We've got to stop and get the top up on this thing."

He halted the jeep. The flash of his brake lights was all the signal the convoy of pickup trucks behind him needed to grind to a standstill.

"Sheryl Lee, if you wouldn't mind, pass the word to the others to double-check the tarps covering their cargo," Charlie said. "Last thing we want is for that storm to ruin all we're haulin'."

The redhead nodded and swung out of the jeep to trot back to the line of pickups. Doors creaked open as drivers stepped down to recheck the ropes that lashed tarpaulins on top of the beds of their vehicles.

Rick's attention turned to the task at hand, aiding Charlie as he unbundled the canvas top and stretched the accordion of metal and fabric over the jeep. Once it was in place, the two secured a series of snaps that anchored the top to the jeep's body.

"Won't keep all the water out when that mother of storms hits, but we'll stay ninety percent dry," Charlie shouted over the now howling wind. He waved Sheryl Lee back to the jeep. "Guess we can't ask for more'n that."

"The storm will make it harder for the Visitors," Rick answered, climbing into the jeep.

Throughout the preceding day, he had heard the whine of skyfighters streaking through the West Texas skies. Since the journey to Dallas had begun two hours and forty miles ago, he had spotted the alien crafts on ten occasions, their daylight-bright searchlights flooding the ground below them.

He had noticed Sheryl Lee's and Charlie's eyes dart to the beams that sliced through the night. Although neither said anything, he knew that their thoughts were the same as his. The Visitors were looking for something, and the odds were that something stemmed from the discovery of *Wanda Sue* and the skyfighter Charlie had shot down.

"Might hinder the lizards; then again it might not." Charlie helped Sheryl Lee inside, then held the canvas-flap door on the passenger side while she zipped it closed. He circled the vehicle and ducked inside, zipping his own door closed. "One thing I *can* tell you: that storm ain't going to help *us* one damned bit. Going's been rough enough without having rain and wind to contend with."

Charlie understated their progress over the plains, Rick thought. Rough didn't begin to describe the snaillike pace at which they crawled over the endless gullies and ravines that time, wind, and water cut into the land east of the Caprock. Twice the winch on the back of the jeep had been employed to pull trucks up inclines too steep for them to climb under their own power.

Four times Charlie's route had taken them across highways, but never along one of the ribbons of concrete and asphalt. Roads were far too dangerous for travel with so many Visitor ships around. The desire for speed gave way to self-preservation; the convoy cut its own trail across rugged, open country, a route made doubly treacherous by the fact they ran without lights.

"Give 'em a flash and let's see how much ground we can cover 'fore the flood hits." Charlie switched on the ignition while Rick dug a flashlight from the toolbox and gave a quick flash behind to signal the others that they were under way again.

The jeep's fabric cover obscured most of the fireworks lighting the heavens ahead of them. Still, Rick saw ragged legs of lightning dance downward to tickle the prairie with their fiery touch. Had it not been for the rain held in those mountainous clouds, he was certain flames rather than water would be the problem confronting the caravan.

"Mother of God!" The profanity burst from Charlie's lips. "Here it comes!"

There was no mist, no preliminary drops of tentative rain. A solid sheet of water struck the jeep, sending a quake through the vehicle's frame.

Charlie's left hand snaked out and found the windshield-wiper knob and pulled and twisted it to high speed. The rubber blades raking against glass did little. The instant they swept away a sheet of water, another deluge washed over the windshield.

"I can barely see two feet ahead of us!" Charlie eased his foot from the gas pedal. The jeep crawled rather than rolled.

Rick couldn't see the two feet Charlie claimed. Even pressing his forehead against the canvas door's plastic windows did nothing to increase visibility. All he saw was rain.

"We could stop and wait until it passes," Sheryl Lee suggested.

"That could be hours!" Charlie's voice came like a low growl. "If we stop here, we're sittin' ducks for those snakes flyin' overhead."

"Better than drivin' blind into a gully." The redhead's tone attempted to soothe the old man's frustration. "I don't want us gettin' killed, not when you've found a way to get the supplies into Dallas."

"I think she's right, Charlie," Rick added. "We can wait and see if the storm lets up."

Charlie nodded, giving in without further protest. He tapped the brake several times to make sure that those behind saw his signal. As the jeep rolled to a stop, he lifted his arms and hooked them over the steering wheel. "We'll give it a half hour or so."

Rick studied the veteran fighter pilot as the older man sat there, shoulders slumped and eyes focused on the torrents that washed down the windshield. For the first time since the young Californian had seen the man drive up in the jeep while they crouched behind the trunks of bushy mesquites, Charlie Scoggin looked old.

"Another fence, Surfer Boy. Your turn." Sheryl Lee scooted around in the jeep's seat, smiled sweetly, and batted her eyelashes in mock innocence before handing him the wire cutters.

"Something tells me I should have kept closer count. This five-for-you, one-for-me mathematics of yours is a bit lopsided," Rick grumbled as he stuffed the cutters in a back pocket.

Swinging around as Charlie drew the jeep to a halt, Rick unzipped a rear opening in the vehicle's canvas top and slid out feet first. The soles of his shoes settled on rain-soggy ground, and he stood. And got a face full of mesquite limb for his trouble.

Growling a string of profanities that would have made a seaman blush, he pushed three other bushy limbs aside and made his way around the jeep through the pelting rain. In the darkness, the storm clouds having obscured the moon's faint light, he found the wire fence barring their progress with only a minor nick to his left thumb from one of the nasty pointed barbs.

"Damned bob wire! Should've kept the open range!" he growled, imitating Charlie's grumble when they had encountered the first in a series of twenty fences three hours ago. "Bob wire! Christ! You've only been in this godforsaken state for two days and you're talking like them. Bob wire—it's *barbed* wire!"

He sheared through the first strand of wire and cursed again. Not only was he picking up a Texas accent, he was talking to himself. The profanities he spat when he cut the second and third strands were for life in general and the twisted quirks it had neatly provided. Quirks that jerked him away from Los Angeles and hurled him down here in the middle of nowhere, sloshing ankle deep in mud while a man who kept a World War II fighter plane in his garage led a modern wagon train across the plains.

Gathering the springy coils of wire from the ground, he dragged them safely to one side so that the jeep might proceed. Charlie didn't stop as he passed through the severed fence. Rick had to trot after the jeep and throw himself through the back opening.

The ludicrous situation would have made a perfect plot for a Cary Grant adventure-comedy, he thought as he toweled his hair to merely wet rather than soaked on a work rag he found tossed in a corner of the back of the jeep. While his clothes remained soaked, at least water wasn't dripping into his face.

Sheryl Lee's decision to wait out the storm had been the correct one. After twenty minutes the wall of water slackened to a simple downpour. Moving out at an average speed of ten miles an hour, the old fighter pilot had somehow managed to keep the convoy on a generally easterly heading while avoiding the creek after creek that had raged with flood-swollen waters.

"I think I see stars up ahead." Sheryl Lee leaned forward and pressed her face to the windshield. "Think this is finally clearin'?"

"Best pray that it is. We've got to make Palo Pinto or Parker County before sunrise," Charlie said. "That is, if we want to find enough timber to hide these pickups under durin' the day."

Rick remembered the road map Charlie had shown him before the trek began. Both counties he mentioned were directly west of Fort Worth. Charlie had explained that the Brazos River cut through the two counties and that forested areas grew near the river. It was these forests, the Cross Timbers region, that would conceal the caravan from the Visitors during the day.

A splatter of water on his left hand drew the young resistance fighter's attention to the opening he had left unzipped. Reaching for the flapping door of cloth and plastic, he groaned. A plaintive horn sounded from the line of trucks behind them.

"Sounds like one of the trucks is in trouble, son." Charlie braked and turned to Rick. "Want to go give it a look-see?"

Rick swallowed the disgruntled reply that danced on the tip of his tongue. Swinging back out the open flap of canvas, he trotted through the rain. He found the problem three trucks beyond the fence he had just cut. A two-tone Dodge pickup rocked back and forth with its right rear wheel up to the axle in mud. There was no way the driver was going to rock the vehicle free of the entrapping mud.

Rapping on the hood as he approached the truck's cab, Rick waited until the window rolled halfway down before saying, "We'll have to push you out of this. Can one of you climb out and give me a hand?"

"Right with you, young feller," Emmett Voss' voice came from the cab's interior darkness. "Netty, take the wheel. Gun it when I call out."

The cab door swung open, and Emmett stepped out while his wife slid behind the wheel. Together he and Rick walked behind the truck to brace themselves at each side of the tailgate.

"On three, Netty," the rancher called to his wife. "One . . . two . . . three!"

Rick threw back and shoulders into the task. The truck's motor raced; the pickup inched forward and abruptly rolled from the mud hole. Simultaneously, Rick's feet flew out from under him, depositing him facedown in the mud.

A misadventure-comedy, he corrected his earlier evaluation of the eastward journey while he pulled himself from the muck and turned his face to the sky to let the still-falling rain wash away his mud mask.

Four hours after the storm struck, the clouds abruptly vanished, leaving a sky sprinkled with the brightest stars Rick had ever seen stretching overhead. The rocky, ravine-ridden terrain that had slowed the caravan's pace to that of a turtle gradually flattened to rolling prairie. Or what had once been rolling prairie. Now most of the land through which Charlie drove was wheat fields.

At least what Texans call wheat fields, Ricky mentally grumbled. Ankle-high stalks covered the land for as far as he could see in all directions. He had seen movies and pictures of wheat fields, wind gently rippling across them so that the vegetation looked like a sea of golden brown. These stunted shafts came closer to being cultivated weeds.

"This all used to be cattle country," Charlie said. He had gradually brought their speed up to twenty miles an hour as the terrain grew more hospitable. "Back in the late seventies a new type of wheat was tried out and it took to this semi-arid climate. Even the big ranches put a portion of their acreage in wheat. Sort of a hedge against the fluctuating cattle market."

"With luck the open fields will cut down on the flat tires," Sheryl Lee said, her gaze surveying what terrain was visible in the darkness.

"That would be a godsend," Rick replied with a weary sigh.

Jagged rocks had claimed two tires while the pickups maneuvered through the ravine country. Rick tried not to think about the rest of the tires on the trucks. Tread was wishful thinking on at least five and almost ancient history on four others. Auto parts, even something as common as tires, were rare in a region where constant skyfighter patrols cut off supplies.

"We can expect fairly easy goin' until we hit the Cross Timbers region." Charlie twisted in his seat to stare out the plastic window at the rear of the jeep. "Only thing botherin' me is the trail we're cuttin' through these fields."

Rick's gaze followed that of the older man. An icy shiver worked up his spine. Two highly visible ruts marked the path the jeep sliced amid the wheat stalks. Seven trucks would widen and deepen the ruts. If the airborne Visitor patrols they sighted earlier had indeed been searching for them, the trail would be a dead giveaway to their route.

"What can we do about it?" Rick glanced back at Charlie.

The Texan pursed his lips and shook his head as he glanced at the ruts again. "Ain't much we can do. Just hope we can cover our trail again when we reach Cross—"

"Charlie!"

Sheryl Lee's scream jerked the two men's heads around. A gully fifteen feet wide loomed just beyond the hood of the jeep. The night and the flatness of the field had cloaked the treacherous trench.

Charlie wrenched the steering wheel to the right.

Too late!

The jeep's front left wheel dropped over the edge of the gully. A pounding heartbeat later, the rest of the vehicle followed the wheel down into the yawning chasm.

Rick's stomach leaped toward his throat. The jeep fell nose first, slowly tilting forward in the darkness. The Californian felt his body lift and float upward, weightless, as the jeep plummeted.

In the next instant the front tires plowed into solid earth. Rick flew through the air until his shoulder collided with the back of Charlie's seat.

The rear of the jeep dropped and bounced. Bone-jarring shudders ran through the vehicle's frame. Rick spilled into the back of the jeep, burying the sharp edges of the toolbox in his side. He groaned and someone whimpered above him. His head turned to find Sheryl Lee hanging draped over the back of her seat.

Still the jeep's motor purred and the four-wheel-drive vehicle moved. *We're bouncing along the bottom of the gully*. The realization somehow penetrated the confusion whirling in his head.

"Hot damn!" Charlie roared with relief. "Don't ask me how, but we're still alive and in one piece!"

Rick managed to right himself as Sheryl Lee slumped back into her seat. Outside, the walls of the gully rose ten feet above the top of the jeep.

The scream of twisting metal and shattering glass rent the night.

"My God!" Charlie's foot jammed the brake to the floorboard.

Rick twisted about. Behind the jeep he saw the dark form of a pickup overturned in the gully. In their own fall he had completely forgotten about the convoy of trucks that blindly followed them.

Ignoring the aches and bruises nagging at his body, Rick scrambled from the back of the jeep and ran sloshing through the water and mud at the bottom of the ditch. Above him he heard the squeal of brakes. He glanced up. The second truck in the caravan halted precariously close to the edge of the gully.

"Back! Back up before the wall gives way!" he shouted, and waved his arms at the pickup.

The driver above responded with a grinding of gears. He shifted into reverse and gunned his motor. The pickup disappeared behind the wall of earth rising above the young resistance fighter. A moment later the distinct metallic crunch of clashing bumpers sounded above the racing motor.

Rick didn't need to see to know what had happened. The truck had plowed into the front of the pickup following it. It didn't matter. A fender was nothing compared to the possibility of having two trucks piled on top of each other in the bottom of the gully.

A moan came from the interior of the overturned pickup when Rick reached its side. Grabbing the passenger door with both hands, he tugged. The door opened two inches, then stopped. Another tug and the door creaked three inches wider. More pained groans came from inside.

Then Charlie was there, reaching out and grasping the twisted edge of the door. "Together. We can get it open."

Rick nodded and pulled, with Charlie adding his strength to the task. Metal on metal ground in a tortured protest; the door swung open. Losing his balance in the mud, Rick tumbled in the darkness and dropped to his backside. Charlie fell into the mud beside him.

"Dad, my dad." A boy no more than fifteen years old spilled from the pickup. "My dad's hurt bad. You got to get him out. He's hurt real bad."

"Is everyone all right down there?" a man called from the top of the gully.

Rick glanced up at the lip of the trench and saw a gathering crowd silhouetted against the sky as the drivers abandoned their trucks and rushed to the accident. He ignored them and picked himself up from the mud to follow Charlie back to the overturned truck's open cab.

While Sheryl Lee knelt beside the boy, Charlie ducked inside. Rick watched while the older man reached out a hand and touched the neck of a man hanging upside down over the truck's steering wheel.

"If you can reach him, we can get him out," Rick said.

"There's no reason to move him, son," Charlie said in a grim whisper. His hand came away from the man's neck moist and dark. "Ben's head went through the windshield. There ain't much left of his neck."

The veteran fighter pilot backed away from the cab and stared at the youth in Sheryl Lee's arms. His chest heaved, then sagged before he knelt and gently told the boy his father was no more.

"No," the boy shouted, attempting to deny reality. "It can't be, Charlie. It can't be."

"There's nothing that can be done for him," Charlie

answered. "And we can't stay, Billy. We've got to move from here. It ain't the way none of us want it, but it's the way it has to be."

The boy's sobs drowned further denial. His head nodded, and he let Charlie help him from the ground and lead him toward the jeep.

"We're not goin' anywhere yet." This from Sheryl Lee, who stood and stared at Charlie. "We have to salvage what supplies we can from the back of the truck."

Charlie turned. Even in the night's blackness, Rick could discern the glare of the man's eyes.

"You said it yourself, Charlie Scoggin." Sheryl Lee stood firm. "Maybe not in the same words, but the meanin' was the same. These medical supplies are more important than all of us. They've got to get through to Fort Worth and Dallas."

Rick's gaze shifted to the overturned truck. Its rear end lay halfway up the opposite side of the gully. Three feet of clearance showed under most of the truck's bed. The supplies could be salvaged.

"She's right, Charlie," a woman said from above. "Ben didn't die so that we could give his load to the snakes."

A mumble of agreement moved through the others standing at the top of the gully. One by one, men and women began to pick their way down the steep incline. A knife came from a pocket and severed one of the cords holding the tarpaulin to the truck's bed. Within minutes boxes were being passed from hand to hand up the gully wall and added to the loads in the trucks above.

The purples and grays of predawn gave way to a golden rose on the eastern horizon. Rick tossed a bushy cedar branch to Emmet Voss, who placed it on the bed of his pickup.

"That should do it." The rancher gave the concealed

truck a final onceover. "Now all we have to do is pray the lizards don't notice us from the air."

Rick nodded, his gaze moving over the small forest of cedars. The break was no more than a thicket of closely packed trees, none growing over fifteen feet into the air. He had never seen vegetation so dense. It was as if the cedars fought one another for possession of the sandy soil that anchored them.

Here and there clearings did open among the cedars. To walk beyond these small patches of sand and rock, a person had to battle his way through a barrier of furry green branches. If he wasn't careful within the break, it would be easy for him to lose his sense of direction and become lost in a matter of seconds, Rick realized.

"This cedar break should keep us all hidden," Charlie replied, tossing another limb into the pickup. "You and the missus get what sleep you can. Things start gettin' tough tonight."

Start getting tough! Rick grimaced while he examined the cedar break that rose about him. *And I thought tonight was bad.*

True to Charlie Scoggin's plan, the convoy had made the Brazos River, although the veteran fighter pilot wasn't certain whether they were in Palo Pinto or Parker County. He had led the trucks into this dense break of cedars and ordered his companions to park beneath the overgrown tree shrubs, then cut limbs with which to conceal their vehicles from any Visitor patrols that might pass overhead.

"It will get tougher," Charlie said in a low voice as he and Rick walked to where Sheryl Lee and Billy Jennings waited beside a jeep heaped with cedar limbs. "A damn sight tougher than anybody expects."

Charlie then explained that if his calculations were correct, the caravan was a mere ninety minutes from the Fort Worth city limits. "The rest of the drive will have to be on roads. Startin' with the one we find to get us across the river.''

Drawing a deep breath, Charlie let it hiss slowly through his teeth. "I don't like bein' in the open like that, but I can't see any way round it. We're runnin' out of country, with nothin' but city ahead.''

Rick didn't know what to say as he slipped into the jeep. Like everyone else in the caravan, he was in Charlie Scoggin's hands. *Even more so,* he thought while he tried to clear a spot in the back of the jeep to stretch out on. *I haven't the slightest idea what Fort Worth or Dallas even looks like.* Somehow he doubted that the city once portrayed by television's prime-time soap opera *Dallas* was the city he hoped to live to see.

As Billy Jennings made his own nest among the junk scattered over the back of the jeep, Rick folded an arm beneath his head to use as a pillow and closed his eyes.

The whine of a Visitor squad vehicle sliced through the silence of the cedar break.

Rick's eyes opened, and he stared at the jeep's top. Not one but two of the lizards' ships passed overhead, moving from south to north. When the telltale high-pitched squeal of their gravity-defying engines faded in the distance, he slowly released an overly held breath. They had passed by without noticing the caravan hidden below.

Charlie's gaze caught and held Rick's for several long moments. Although neither spoke, Rick knew the older man silently whispered the same prayer that moved through his mind—that the alien ships were merely on routine patrol and not searching for *Wanda Sue*'s missing cargo and passengers.

Chapter 14

Houston Mother Ship Commander Garth's strides were brisk and sharp as he walked past the smoking ruins that had housed the South Fort Worth Processing Center only two hours ago.

In spite of the early morning hour and the fact he had been dragged from a sound sleep to make the flight to Fort Worth, he maintained a strict military facade, one that bespoke strength and dignity. At the moment it was all he had to boost the morale of those who had fallen in defeat at the hands of resistance fighters.

"A total of seventy-four of our forces died in the explosions," a raven-haired lieutenant walking beside him said, rattling off the final tallies of the battle. "Included in those dead were the center's Captain Maureen. Another twenty-five shock troopers were injured. . . ."

At least the officer in command had the decency to die in the fray, Garth thought with little comfort. Perhaps if the facts of what had happened here last night were bent a bit here, molded a little there, the captain's death and those of her troops could be used. He would have to pass the seed of an idea blossoming in his mind along to his staff. The troops needed heroes who willingly sacrificed their lives to glorify the Great Leader and his cause.

"Engineering estimates it will take at least two weeks until another processing center is fully operational," the lieutenant continued. "They suggest a site in an abandoned shopping mall about two miles to the southwest."

Two nights ago the processing center in Dallas' Cotton Bowl had been destroyed. And now this! Garth's chest tightened. Something was up. Why had these human animals become so restless?

"Should I tell Engineering to proceed with construction of the new center?"

"Wha— Yes, yes immediately," Garth replied, irritated by the break in his train of thought. "Lieutenant, it's my understanding two members of the resistance were captured during last night's attack."

"Yes, sir." The young woman looked up at her commanding officer. "Major Lawrence is presently questioning the pair."

"I want to see them," Garth said.

"They've been taken to Fort Worth Processing Center Two," the woman answered, as though taken totally off guard by the request.

"Then I suggest that we are wasting valuable time remaining here, Lieutenant." Garth turned and walked to his waiting squad vehicle.

They're merely children! Garth studied the faces that glared at him. Neither could be more than fifteen human years in age. Yet such hate twisted their dirty faces.

However, not even the hate could conceal the fear he detected. Like an ugly little worm, it wiggled just below the surface of their defiant masks. Both the captives had reason to fear.

"Major Lawrence, show them the photograph of the woman I seek," Garth said.

The officer extracted a color photograph from the breast pocket of his uniform and shoved it into the faces of his two captives.

A hint of a smile lifted the corners of Garth's mouth.

They both knew the bitch's offspring. Although neither spoke, he saw it in the way their eyes widened.

"Major, begin with the female's hands," Garth ordered. "Work upward until the bones of the arms are splinters, then move on to the legs if necessary."

Garth pivoted, walked from the interrogation room, and exited the processing center, leaving Major Lawrence to his pleasures. Outside, the Texas sun already burned like an inferno in the sky, and it was only nine in the morning. Even with the dark glasses he wore, the alien could only tolerate staring directly into its face a fraction of a second.

The hum of an approaching squad vehicle pulled his attention to the north. He watched the craft settle atop a bulls-eye painted on the pavement to his left. The ship's side door opened, its lower half swinging down to form an exit ramp.

The first of the day's harvest, he thought while shock troopers prodded the human cargo from the interior of the ship and marched them into the processing center. *Production will have to be increased here to make up for last night's disaster.*

His gaze moved from the line of humans who shuffled in a drugged stupor toward the cold sleep awaiting them. The blasted ruins of what had once been Carswell Air Force Base surrounded him. Here were the seared skeletons of B-52 bombers, destroyed before the awkward craft could lift off from their runways.

The site for the processing center was perfect. It served as a constant reminder to the humans that their resistance to Visitor domination was futile. How could they expect to be victorious when this bastion of their military might had been so easily destroyed?

A cold finger tapped at his spine. Yet the humans did continue to struggle. The ruins of two processing centers were harsh testimony to just how effective their tactics could be.

No, Garth shook his head. The human resistance fighters had gained nothing with their terroristic assaults on the centers. They only delayed the inevitable. The delay was minor in the overall scheme of the Great Leader's plan for conquest. In the end every human being in both Dallas and Fort Worth, as well as those in the suburbs surrounding the cities, would one day shuffle his or her way into a processing center to sleep the cold sleep until the final fate of each was decided.

"Commander Garth."

Major Lawrence's voice wedged into the commander's thoughts. Garth turned to see his fellow officer walk from the processing center.

"You were correct in beginning the interrogation with the girl." Lawrence grinned. "While she refused to do more than scream even as I started on her second arm, the male could not endure her suffering."

Garth smiled. "And?"

"This female is Sheryl Lee Darcy." Major Lawrence pointed to the photograph he still held. "She is the daughter of the resistance leader who died in Dallas yesterday."

"I know that much, Major." Garth grew impatient. "Did the boy know anything else?"

"This Sheryl Lee Darcy and a companion are presently on a mission to secure medical supplies for the resistance forces in this sector," the major continued. "The male knew nothing more except that she left this region more than a week ago."

Garth's smile grew. How neatly the pieces fell into place. Not only had the woman been aboard the downed airplane discovered near Lubbock, but the plane had carried medical supplies. Both woman and cargo were now missing.

If the daughter has half the spirit of the mother, then she will find—has found—a method of transporting those supplies into this sector, Garth silently speculated. His alien pulse quickened. *Even now she comes to me. I can feel it!*

"The male also provided me with the location of the Fort Worth resistance headquarters," Major Lawrence continued. "I have ordered an immediate raid."

"Good, good, Major," Garth said, although he knew the raid would prove fruitless. Fearing that the captives might reveal their location, resistance leaders would have moved to a secondary hiding place by the time Major Lawrence's shock troopers arrived. Still, he would accompany the major, just in case.

It didn't matter to Garth. The Fort Worth resistance was of little concern to him, not with the bitch's offspring so near.

"Major, I will require quarters here in Fort Worth for the next few days. You will arrange something for me?" Garth asked.

"My own quarters within the processing center are yours for as long as you desire, Commander," the major answered. "Shall I escort you to them?"

"In a moment, Major, but first I need to communicate with the Mother Ship," Garth answered. "I want to triple the aerial patrols between the Fort Worth and Lubbock sectors."

Chapter 15

Rick awoke feeling like he had spent the night—
no, day, he corrected himself—in a Turkish steam bath.
He stretched and rammed a knee into the back of an
unyielding jeep seat. Grunting a curse, he rolled to the
side to escape the obstacle and rammed his left elbow
against the sharp-edged toolbox.

"Shh." Sheryl Lee looked at him and placed a finger
to her lips. "Billy's still sleepin'."

Rolling his eyes to the side, Rick saw the teenager
curled into a ball tucked into a rear corner of the vehicle.
The Californian looked back at his redheaded companion. "Charlie?"

"Outside for the past half hour or so."

Rick untangled legs that ached with two kinks for each
muscle and wiggled into the driver's seat. Harsh sunlight
filtered through the cedar limbs piled over the jeep's
windshield. "What time is it anyway?"

"Three," Sheryl Lee answered while she did her best
to stretch in the jeep's cramped confines. "You look as
bad as I feel."

Rick shrugged. "It comes from good, clean living."
He smiled. In spite of the heat, the humidity, and the
rigors of the past two days, Sheryl Lee remained the
beautiful fiery-tressed angel who had greeted him aboard
the *Wanda Sue.* "Care for a stroll?"

"I'll be out in a little bit," she said, managing a weak
return to his smile. Her emerald eyes turned to the

windshield. She stared, her expression distant and removed. "I need some time to think."

He didn't press further, simply nodded, unzipped the jeep's fabric door, and stepped outside. Squinting against the glaring sunlight, he found Charlie seated on the ground, half hidden among the furry branches of a clump of cedars. The older man looked up and waved a greeting.

Rick surveyed his surroundings. The bushy trees looked more dwarfed in daylight than they had in the morning grays. Once again he was struck by how thickly the cedars grew, like impenetrable walls of green.

He stretched and drew a deep breath. His nose wrinkled. The smell of the stunted trees was overwhelming in the moist heat, approximating the pungency of a cat's litter box that hadn't been changed in weeks.

"Whew!" He tried to shake away the odor. There was no escape.

"You'll get used to it in a moment or two, I reckon." Charlie chuckled. "That is, if it doesn't kill you first."

Rick grimaced. "I think it might be . . ."

The rest of his sentence was left unspoken. The high-pitched hum of approaching Visitor ships came from the west. Rick darted beside Charlie and squatted among the prickly limbs. Two low-flying skyfighters shot overhead.

"Dreamed they were buzzing us all day," Rick said, stepping out to examine a cloudless sky.

"You weren't dreamin'." Charlie pulled a dry blade of grass from the ground and chewed on it. "They woke me four times today. And that's the second time they've been over since I got up."

"Same ships?"

"Hard to tell. Snakes don't go in for markin' their craft that much. But I'd lay odds it's the same pair." Charlie tugged the grass from his mouth, studied it a moment, then slipped it back between his lips. "They're lookin' for us, you know."

"Yeah, I figured that out last night. They found the *Wanda Sue* and the skyfighter you brought down." Rick turned back to his companion. "You've done a hell of a job keeping them off our backs so far."

"Wish Ben Jennings was here to say that." Charlie's chest heaved and his head moved wearily from side to side. "If we can just hold out here 'til dark, we've got a chance of makin' it into Fort Worth. With luck we just might be able to keep our hides in one piece while doin' it."

Rick pursed his lips. "Then you weren't just talking last night when you said it was going to be tough."

"I wasn't bullin' you, son," Charlie said. "Things are liable to get a mite ticklish the moment we pull out of here."

Rick's gaze lifted back to the cloudless blue. "Ticklish" wasn't the term he would have used—not with the Visitors swarming the sky in search of them. The truth was, he might very well die on this insane cross-Texas run, a fact that offered him no comfort.

"Either of you happen to think of bringin' food along on this little jaunt?" Sheryl Lee's head poked above the cedar limbs atop the jeep.

"Water's in a couple canteens stuffed under the driver's seat," Charlie replied. "But I'm afraid I forgot to bring so much as a candy bar. If you ain't particularly choosy, there's some wild persimmons and a few ripe pecans down by the river. Not much, but it'll stop your stomach from complainin'."

"Feel like that stroll now, Surfer Boy?" The young woman looked at Rick.

"Why not?" He shrugged. "Let me get my weapons."

Walking back to the jeep, he ducked inside and pulled the Uzi and energy pistol from the back. The pockets of Sheryl Lee's khaki jump suit were already weighted with the two pistols she carried.

"You two be careful," Charlie called after them as they started eastward through the cedar break. "It's still warm and this is copperhead country."

Rick warily glanced about him. "I thought Texas had rattlesnakes."

"And copperheads, water moccasins, and coral snakes." Sheryl Lee grinned. "Not to mention a variety of poisonous spiders, cougars, wolves, bears, and bobcats. But don't worry, Surfer Boy, I won't let you get snake bit. However, if it comes to any of the others, you're on your own."

"Great." He couldn't tell whether she was just stating a fact or was taking advantage of a gullible greenhorn.

The cedar break gave way to a dense forest of stunted gnarled trees Sheryl Lee called red oaks and a profusion of underbrush that seemed to have but one thing in common—thorns. Picking a path of least resistance, they walked a half mile before coming to a swollen, muddy stream perhaps twenty feet from one bank to the other. Trees, real trees, not the overgrown shrubs Rick had seen since the *Wanda Sue* had crashed, grew thick and green along the banks.

"The Brazos River." Sheryl Lee waved a hand at the brown current of water.

"I thought things were big in Texas." Rick eyed the stream. "Do you call lakes oceans?"

An expression of disgust on her face, Sheryl Lee perused the vegetation along the bank. "There's the persimmons Charlie mentioned. And this is a pecan tree."

Charlie had understated the case when it came to the pecans. Neither Rick nor Sheryl Lee found one mature enough to eat. Rick dubiously eyed the brown-black ball the redhead handed him and tasted the giant marble-sized wild persimmon only after the young woman took the first bite. The brown pulpy fruit was a warm, tasteless sweet—more pit than meat. However, after ten of them his stomach did stop its rumbling.

"Not exactly Charlie's steak and eggs, is it?" Sheryl Lee spat a pit to the ground. "Better than nothing, I guess."

"It'll have to do until we reach your friends in Fort Worth." Rick picked a double handful of the persimmons and stuffed them into an empty jacket pocket.

A frown darkened Sheryl Lee's face. Rick stared at her. "Anything the matter?"

"My friends are in Dallas. And they're expecting the medical supplies to arrive by air, not in pickup trucks," she started, then fell silent.

The whine of Visitor ships came from the sky.

Grabbing Sheryl Lee's arm, Rick tugged her beneath the pecan tree's leafy boughs. Above, two skyfighters slowly skimmed the top of the stunted forest. They disappeared on an eastward course, but the hum of their engines hung in the air.

"Something's up." Rick's mind raced, imagining a hundred disastrous scenarios. "Wait here."

Cautiously he crept from under the pecan and worked around a dense clump of red oaks. A half mile northeast of the river the two alien ships hovered in midair.

"What is it?" Sheryl Lee abandoned the pecan tree and moved to his side. He didn't answer. She saw the skyfighters and asked, "What are they doin'?"

"Your guess is as good as mine." Rick stared at the two ships. "They're north of the camp. If they spotted . . ."

The skyfighters sank toward the ground. The forest swallowed their white segmented bodies. The whine of the gravity-defying engines died.

"Rick, they *did* sight the camp!" Sheryl Lee's hand closed around his arm and squeezed. "We've got to warn the others!"

The Californian didn't argue or mention that she had called him by name for the first time since they met. Instead, he ran at her side as she darted through the tangle of vines and undergrowth toward the cedar break.

A cry—a human cry—rent the woods. The thunderous blast of a shotgun drowned the cry.

"God! They've found the camp." Panic tightened the young woman's voice when they reached the edge of the cedar break.

Rifle and shotgun reports echoed constantly now, leaving no doubt that the convoy of pickup trucks had been discovered and was now under attack.

Rick found their own tracks leading from the cedars and motioned to his companion. "We won't do any good rushing in there. We have to take it slow and easy—see if we can maneuver behind the snakes. Keep low."

With that, he entered the closely packed trees. Sound rather than sight guided his movements. Even amid the bark of rifles and shotguns, he could discern the harsh sizzle of discharged energy bolts.

"I can't see anything but trees," Sheryl Lee whispered. "Dammit, we should be right on top of the fightin'!"

He agreed. But the cedars grew so close it was impossible to see either man or alien.

Another human scream wailed.

"There!" Rick saw an overall-clad farmer drop from behind a bushy wall of green.

The man writhed at the edge of a sandy clearing, hands clutching his stomach. Three quick bursts of blue-white erupted from the opposite side of the clearing and lanced into the moaning rancher like spears of light. The wounded man jerked spasmodically, then lay dead still.

Jerking the Uzi to shoulder height, the resistance fighter pointed the barrel at the barrier of branches hiding the source of blasts. His finger squeezed the trigger. Splintered green and brown flew into the air when the twenty-round burst tore into the cedars.

And a scream—an alien scream—mingled with the rifle reports. A red-uniformed, helmeted shock trooper staggered into the sandy opening between the cedars. Two moist blossoms of blood spread along the left sleeve of his uniform. He swayed from side to side, his energy rifle raised to face an invisible enemy.

The crackle of unleashed power came from Rick's side. Sheryl Lee stood and fired. The bolts from her stolen weapon struck straight and true. A hissing death cry tore from behind the black face mask of the shock trooper's helmet. The alien soldier's body flew across the clearing under the impact of the blasts.

In the next instant Sheryl Lee ducked. Red flashed to her left, then blue-white. Searing balls of energy, like fiery pearls, hissed through empty air.

The Visitor volley received a double-barreled reply. No more than five feet from where Rick had seen the patch of red uniform, a 12-gauge shotgun opened up with both barrels blazing yellow and blue.

There was no death scream this time. The alien body that crumpled to the ground had no head.

"Got one of the bastards!" a woman called out. "That's two of the—"

A barrage of energy beams coming from three direc· tions sliced into the cedars, homing in on the voice that changed into a bloody scream. Deer rifles from as many sources answered the Visitor attack.

"Sweet Jesus," Rick hissed through clenched teeth as he emptied the Uzi and snapped in another clip. "This is sheer chaos. Charlie and the others are scattered through the trees."

"So are the Visitors." Sheryl Lee was on her stomach, peering beneath the busy branches of the cedars. "Which means the lizards are just as confused as we are. Come on, we aren't doing any good here."

On her belly the redhead crawled forward between one of the cedars. Rick dropped to the ground and wiggled beside her. It wasn't the most graceful position he had ever been in, but at the moment, with human and alien ready to shoot anything that moved, it was the safest.

Together they reached another of the sandy clearings.

To their left Rick saw mounds of cedar limbs concealing two pickups. Barrels of deer rifles poked through the cut branches.

"To the right." Sheryl Lee nudged his side and tilted her head toward the opposite side of the clearing. "There at the base of the trees."

A humorless smile played at the corners of the Californian's mouth. He sighted a pair of black boots and the red uniform tucked into their tops.

"Bring him out and I'll take him." Sheryl Lee lifted her energy pistol.

Rick complied. He squeezed the machine pistol's trigger, spraying the Teflon-coated bullets in a low, tight-knit pattern. Sheryl Lee never got the opportunity to fire. When the Visitor burst from his hiding place, three deer rifles blazed. The shock trooper's face mask exploded in a shower of dark splinters as slugs of lead sought vulnerable reptilian flesh beneath.

"Human scum!"

A feral hiss-growl came from behind Rick. He rolled onto his back. A shock trooper stood five feet away, energy rifle raised and ready.

The young resistance fighter reacted rather than thought. Shoving Sheryl Lee aside, he rolled in the opposite direction. The alien's weapon sizzled. Searing heat fused the sand where he had lain but a fraction of a second ago.

As he landed on his back for a second time, he wrenched the Uzi high. His trigger finger squeezed. The machine pistol's firing pin clicked on an empty chamber.

Before he grasped what happened, the deafening thunder of an exploding shotgun came from the Visitor's left. At the same time, Sheryl Lee opened up with her energy pistol.

There was no escape from the crossfire of buckshot and deadly bolts. The reptilian warrior's body was lifted from the ground and thrown into five cedars behind him. When he dropped, it was never to rise again.

"That's four of the bastards." Charlie Scoggin pushed through thick limbs with a still-smoking shotgun in his hands. "There's four more—"

A volley of shots and a barrage of energy bolts sounded north of the clearing. Both human and alien yowls of anguish filled the air.

"Maybe less now," Charlie finished as he shrugged and disappeared back into the cedars.

Rick reached for another clip and found only wild persimmons in his pocket. Tossing away the now useless machine pistol, he stood, scooped the dead shock trooper's rifle from the ground, and darted after the older man. Sheryl Lee ran at his heels.

Another exchange of gunfire came ahead of them and more screams.

Fifty feet from the sandy clearing, they found the reason. Two snakes had pinned down five men and women behind three of the pickups. A third Visitor lay dead at his companions' feet.

Charlie pumped a fresh round into his shotgun and raised the weapon. Rick's hand shot up and pulled the barrel downward.

"We'd do more good if we circled around and took them from behind," he said.

Sheryl Lee and Charlie nodded. This time they followed the young Californian as he led them in a wide curving path through the dense cedars. When he stopped, he eased aside the thick branches ahead of him. The two aliens were ten feet away.

Neither shock trooper knew what hit him when two stolen energy weapons and one shotgun poked through the bushy foliage and spoke.

"That's seven," Charlie spat. Then he called out to those in the caravan. "There's one left! Fan out and keep your eyes peeled for the snake. And for the love of God, don't go shootin' each other!"

A rustle of parting branches came from behind the

trio. Rick spun around. A shock trooper strode through the cedars. His rifle's muzzle lifted, homing in on Sheryl Lee's back.

Again the young man reacted rather than thought. Throwing his shoulder into the redhead's side, he sent the woman sprawling to the ground.

A blast of blue-white seared over his left hip, scorching the fabric of his blue jeans as he tumbled in the cedars after Sheryl Lee. Falling, he jerked up the barrel to his rifle, pointed in the general direction of the shock trooper, and fired.

The bolt slammed into the Visitor's own weapon. A split second later a portion of hell reigned on earth!

The shock trooper's rifle exploded. In a heartbeat an actinic ball of sizzling white flared, grew, enveloped the alien, and dissipated, leaving a charred, smoldering corpse in its wake.

Rick disentangled himself from Sheryl Lee and pushed to an elbow, his mouth gaping.

"Rick?" Sheryl Lee sat up beside him.

Her arms encircled him as she stared in horror. Beneath the khaki coveralls, shivers of fear and relief quaked through her body. His own arm moved about her slender waist to gently draw her trembling body to his. He turned, his eyes meeting emerald gems that revealed a terror he had never seen in their sparkling inner light.

"Close." Her whisper was a shaky quaver. "I didn't even hear him."

"Shh. It's over now." His head tilted and he lightly kissed her quivering lips. "It's over, and we've come through it in one piece again."

She managed a weak smile as her mouth rose to him once again, lips lightly brushing then clinging to his.

Somewhere in the distant background, Rick heard Charlie grunt, "Eight."

Chapter 16

Rick tried to push aside the image of eight bodies laid beneath the overhanging branches of three stunted cedars. He couldn't. The price the farmers and ranchers had paid to protect the medical supplies had been high. For each Visitor killed, one of them had fallen.

"It don't make sense, Rick." Charlie brushed aside a furry branch, stepped between two cedars, and proceeded northward. "We're still outside the Visitors' safe zone. The red dust should have killed the snakes the moment they stepped out of the skyfighters."

"I know." Rick shook his head. "It should have handled the two in the skyfighter you shot down on the Caprock, but it didn't."

"It just don't make sense—and it cost us eight good men and women! Dammit, that's what hurts the most! Those are my neighbors layin' dead back there. They were my friends!" Anger and pain railed in the older man's voice. Agony twisted the features of his thin face.

"Charlie," Rick said, softening his tone, "they knew the risk in what we're trying to do. They understood the dangers and accepted them. Don't lessen the sacrifice they made."

"I'm not," he answered without glancing at his young companion. "It's just that this whole damned world is out of kilter. Those eight shouldn't be dead. They should be at home with their families, bouncin' grandchildren on their knees. And young folks like Sheryl Lee and yourself should be off makin' grandchildren for old goats like me to spoil."

"In time we'll get back to that," Rick said. "But right now we've got another task at hand."

"Yeah, I know." The heaviness in his words matched the feeling in Rick's chest. "And that job just might kill the rest of us."

Together the two men stepped from the cedar break into a hundred-foot clearing sprinkled with prickly pear. Squatted amid the flat-leafed cactus were two sky-fighters.

"Ugly things, ain't they?" Charlie sucked at his teeth. "Fly like a helicopter, jet, and space shuttle rolled into one, and look like a wingless dragonfly. Think I'll stick with my Mustang, thank you."

"Come on, let's get this over with."

Rick lifted the energy rifle he carried and darted to the side of the first craft, while Charlie shot to the second. They nodded at one another, then ducked inside the ships.

A sigh of relief escaped the Californian's lips when his gaze took in the ship's interior. It was empty. Then he cursed. There were no more weapons inside except for the skyfighter's own armaments. The hike to the ships, at least as far as this one went, had been a waste of time.

Hopeful that Charlie's luck was better than his own, he exited the craft and entered the second. His companion stood over the fighter's controls, staring at the blinking panels of lights. He edged back his cap and scratched his head.

"More complicated than the Mustang's controls, eh?" Rick smiled.

"Well, to tell the truth, I was just thinkin' how familiar all this looks." Charlie turned and grinned at his young friend. "Can't tell a hell of a lot about some of these buttons and switches, but these levers here at the side of the pilot's seat resemble a joystick. Wonder what she flies like?"

"Too bad these aren't squad vehicles." Rick surveyed the cramped interior of the small ship. "With two squad vehicles, we could fly the medical supplies into Fort Worth and Dallas right under the Visitors' noses."

"Now that would make things a mite easier for everyone involved." Charlie lowered himself into the pilot's chair and pressed a glowing yellow button.

"Fort Worth Patrol LBB-2 requests permission to enter next sector," a static-popping voice came from a grille set in a panel directly before the pilot's seat. Another voice answered, "Fort Worth Control affirms negative report of Weatherford search. Permission to continue reconnaissance in the Stephenville sector."

Charlie chuckled. "Now this would be a nice little gem to carry with us. We could keep tabs on everything the snakes were doing in the air."

Rick's eyes shifted between the man and the controls. "Charlie, can you fly this thing?"

The older man's head jerked up, and he stared at his companion. "You're serious, ain't ya?"

"Dead serious," Rick replied. "With one of these, we've got air support for our convoy. Can you fly it?"

For a heavy, silent moment, the old fighter pilot continued to stare. Then with a heave of his chest, he said, "Guess there's only one way to find out. Strap yourself in and keep your fingers crossed. I ain't goin' to guarantee anything except that you're in for an interestin' ride!"

While Rick crossed to the co-pilot's chair, Charlie's fingers moved hesitantly over the control panel. "Here goes nothin'!"

He tapped the largest of a series of green buttons before him. And he was right—nothing happened.

"Let's try the next one," he said as he tapped a smaller green button.

Again nothing happened.

Nor did any of the five green buttons produce a noticeable result. In reverse order, he pressed the buttons again. "I know they have to be for something more than decoration. Now this red one . . ."

A slight vibration ran through the skyfighter the instant he depressed the button. The familiar whine of the craft's engines filled Rick's ears. He glanced at his friend and smiled.

Charlie reached down and grasped the controls to each side of the seat. "I'd feel a mite better if we could close that door back there before tryin' to get this thing off the ground. Give a couple buttons a push."

At random, Rick touched a fingertip to a long blue panel. Two balls of sizzling energy blasted from the skyfighter's duel nose cannons. Rick jerked back. Two more blasts came from the guns. "How? I didn't touch it again."

"These buttons on the control levers," Charlie said with a grin. "System redundancy built into this baby. Try another."

Far more hesitant than on his first try, Rick tapped a round green button. The ship's engines whined down. Immediately, he tapped the button again, and the engines reawoke. He glanced at Charlie again.

"Don't look at me, son. I don't know what the lizard engineers were doin' when they designed this thing." Charlie shrugged. "Keep tryin'."

He did. Another blue button turned off the craft's interior lights. A pink button appeared to do nothing. His fingers skipped over the only black button of the panel to tap a white one that turned on the exterior loudspeakers. Another press turned them off. He reached for a yellow button that blinked alive at his touch—and the door hissed shut.

"It's called flyin' by the seat of your pants." Charlie

grinned. "It worked for ol' Orville and Wilbur. Now let's see if it works for us."

Gently he eased back on the lever to his right. The engine whine doubled its pitch and the ship shuddered but did not move. He pulled back the lever, muttered something about "southpaw lizards," and shifted the left lever slightly. The skyfighter lurched in a little hopping motion. Charlie grunted and worked the two levers together. The ship floated into the air, wobbling from side to side.

"As easy as it looks," he said aloud, although Rick was certain the older man's words were meant as much to reassure himself as to comfort his passenger. "Now let's see what this machine can do!"

An invisible fist slammed into Rick's chest and remained there, forcing him back into the seat's cushioning. Outside, the West Texas forest of oak and cedar was transformed into a green blur.

"Jeb, Billy, Will, pile as many of those branches as you can into the back of the jeep," Charlie shouted to his friends. "We've still got a use for them."

"Fly?" The disbelief in Sheryl Lee's voice matched the doubt on her face. "Charlie can handle a sky-fighter?"

Rick reaffirmed the events of the past half hour with a nod and a grin.

"Like I was born to those controls," Charlie added, his chest swelling. "No wonder the snakes are such good pilots. One of these things practically flies itself. Hell, I could have Rick flyin' one in a day or two."

"And you flew to Fort Worth?"

"What's left of it," Rick answered, trying not to remember the wholesale destruction he had seen during the flyover.

"There's no way into the city except by the main highways. And those are crawlin' with lizards," Charlie said while tossing an armload of cedar branches into the jeep. "That's where the skyfighter comes in. With Rick as tailgunner and me at the controls, we can give you aerial support. Shoot a path through the Visitors."

"And commit suicide in the process, as well as gettin' everyone left in this caravan killed." Sheryl Lee bit at her lower lip. Her reprimanding gaze shifted between the two men. "A head-on blockade run won't work, and both of you know it."

"We've considered that." Rick glanced at Charlie, who nodded. "We can't see any other way of getting into the city. It's an all-or-nothing situation."

"It doesn't have to be." Sheryl Lee rubbed a hand over her brow, pursed her lips, and stared at the ground.

"But you said earlier that the resistance is expecting you from the air, that they aren't ready for an overland convoy," Rick protested.

"Yes, yes, I know. It's been eatin' at me since I woke up this afternoon. I've been tryin' to come up with some way of contactin' my friends." Sheryl Lee's head lifted. "Now Charlie's given me the way to do just that."

Rick frowned, uncertain what the redhead had in mind.

"Are you thinkin' what I think you're thinkin', li'l' lady?" This from Charlie.

Sheryl Lee's head bobbed in affirmation. "If you could fly me into Dallas, I can get us help. Some plan can be worked out that will at least give us a chance of succeedin'."

"You can't be serious." Rick shook his head.

" 'Fraid she is, son." Charlie shrugged. "I think we'd better hide that second skyfighter, then take us another little trip into Fort Worth."

"Dallas," Sheryl Lee corrected.

Chapter 17

Below, six pickup trucks minus Charlie's jeep moved off the highway into an abandoned junkyard on the outskirts of a town that, to Rick, was but a black dot and a name on a map—Mineral Wells.

"They should be safe there until we get back." Charlie glanced at Sheryl Lee in the co-pilot's seat and at Rick, who stood behind her. He then nosed the craft westward.

Rick smiled as the junkyard slipped by beneath them. The automobile graveyard was a stroke of genius on his part, even if he had to admit it himself. Let the snakes scour the countryside for the convoy. They'd never think of looking among the lines of wrecked cars for the mud-splattered pickups, which from the air appeared to be nothing more than junkers.

"Best get on back to the tail," Charlie said, tilting his head to the rear of the alien craft. "With luck, we won't need those rear guns, but . . ."

The older man's words trailed away as Rick turned and took his position as tailgunner. Neither he nor Sheryl Lee needed to be reminded of the ifs and buts surrounding the flight.

Reaching down the left side of the seat, he found a single black switch and flicked it. A series of green-glowing circles and a pair of cross hairs appeared on a mini-display screen that slid from the right arm of the chair, then swung around in front of him. He rested his hands around the firing grips on the seat's arms, then looked out the wide window that filled the rear of the craft.

"I'm slippin' down to pick up Interstate 20," Charlie explained as the ship banked to the south. "We'll follow that into Fort Worth."

Moments later twin ribbons of concrete appeared below. Rick saw little else until the skyfighter sailed above the Fort Worth city limits. The scene outside made no sense. Here was block on block of homes with green lawns and cars parked in their driveways. There, but a street away, lay charred mounds of rubble.

Rick saw no rhyme or reason to the selective destruction the Visitors had wrought on the city. It was as though some madman had randomly decided this portion of the city would live and that portion would die. He sucked at his teeth. Even the insane often had method in their madness. No madman's twisted mind had decreed For Worth's fate—nor had that mind even been human, but an alien brain, a reptilian intelligence born on a planet that circled a sun more than eight light-years from Earth.

"To the north," he heard Sheryl Lee say. "That used to be Carswell Air Force Base. The buildings there at the end of the runway are new. The Visitors have set up a processing center there. They have another on the south side of town. We've taken out four centers in the area already—and still they build them."

Rick saw the swath of scorched earth that surrounded runways pockmarked with blast craters. He remembered Joe Bob mentioning that this had once been a Strategic Air Command base. Now it was an alien meat-packing plant. He closed his eyes and drew a deep, steadying breath.

Garth watched a skyfighter shoot overhead and disappear eastward toward Dallas. His eyes lowered to the line of abandoned shops Major Lawrence had brought him to.

He smiled when his gaze alighted on a shattered sign on the ground before one of the stores. It read FA TAST C W RLDS.

Fantastic Worlds, he mentally filled in the sign's missing letters. Beyond the shop's broken windows were overturned display cases, which gave no hint of the wares a human merchant once peddled within. Which was only the way it should be. Soon this whole planet would be without a trace of the sentient creatures it had given birth to.

"They're gone!" Major Lawrence stepped from the missing doorway of a shop to the right of the sign that held Garth's attention. "But they were here. They left their garbage—cans, bottles, candy wrappers. From the trash piled up, I'd say they'd been hidden inside for at least a week, maybe two."

"But they're gone now." Garth repeated what he had known would be the case. Others might underestimate the human resistance movement, but not him. "A week, maybe two, and so close to our Carswell processing center. Right under your nose, wouldn't you say, Major?"

Major Lawrence stiffened at the accusation but offered no reply.

The fool! he thought, but said, "Never mind, Major. It grows late, and I must get back. The afternoon reports on the search will soon be in. Recall your men. It's time I returned to the processing center."

While the major followed his commander, Garth returned to a squad vehicle and settled into the co-pilot's seat. He had accompanied Lawrence and his men on the slim chance the raid might bear fruit and take him a step closer to the human female he sought. His only possibility of success now lay with the air search that was under way west of the city.

* * *

Even the early evening dusk could not conceal the destruction over which the skyfighter passed. What had once been downtown Dallas was now mountainous mounds of debris.

Twisted metal girders, shattered bricks, and splintered panes of glass covered the ground for as far as Rick could see. He recalled old World War II newsreel footage of bombed-out European cities that he had seen on television. This was worse. In those aging black-and-white films, partially standing buildings and walls were seen. Here it was impossible to even imagine that the rubble had once been skyscrapers, let alone the heart of one of the country's major cities.

How many had died beneath structures toppled by the Visitors' unmerciful assault on Dallas? How many more were daily being shuttled aboard the Visitors' Mother Ships? Rick could only guess. The estimated tally churned his stomach—hundreds of thousands!

"Where should I set us down?" Charlie spoke from the front of the ship.

"Anyplace that looks safe." Sheryl Lee stared at the ruin of what had once been a great city. "We'll have to cover a lot of ground on foot. I don't want to lead the snakes to our headquarters."

"Those miniwarehouses ahead look good. I'll just set us down alongside them. We'll wait for dark before lookin' for your friends." Charlie nosed the skyfighter toward the ground.

A half hour later night covered the city. Three blocks from the warehouses Rick found a dust-covered station wagon. A brick opened the driver's window, and it was a simple matter to hot-wire the car.

"At least we won't have to walk." He grinned and slid across the front seat to the passenger's side, letting Sheryl Lee take the wheel. "It's your show now."

The moment Charlie settled in the backseat, the redhead eased the station wagon into drive and pulled

away from the curb. Without either headlights or
streetlights, Rick could tell very little about the city they
passed through. One thing that did surprise him was the
trees. These were real trees, towering monsters with
thick, solid trunks and lofty branches that often spread
overhead to canopy the streets Sheryl Lee maneuvered
through.

Twice the redhead pulled under the protection of these
leafy boughs and halted to avoid the probing searchlights
of Visitor squad vehicles that passed above. On four
other occasions, she wheeled the station wagon into
shadow-cloaked alleys at the approach of twin headlight
beams that announced the snakes' ground patrols.

After forty-five minutes of weaving her way around
block upon block of total destruction or through streets
littered with abandoned automobiles, Sheryl Lee steered
the station wagon into a parking lot containing row upon
row of deserted eighteen-wheelers, rusting monsters that
once ruled the nation's now barren highways. A sign
partially blasted from a building on the south side of the
lot proclaimed this had once been headquarters for a
trucking company.

"We're northwest of the downtown area," she said as
she opened her door and stepped out. "I don't want to
risk drivin' any closer. We'll have to do the last few
blocks on foot."

Those "few blocks" stretched to ten long ones
through a warehouse district. From shadow to shadow,
they ducked and ran.

Rick's senses were honed to an almost preternatural
sharpness. His eyes and ears were constantly alert for a
movement within the night darkness, the whine of
Visitor ships overhead, the rumble of ground vehicles, or
the snap of a twig or the crunch of gravel underfoot that
would give away the presence of snakes waiting to snare
the careless.

"Just across another street now," Sheryl Lee whis-

pered while she pressed flat against the side of a brick
building and nodded toward an electronics warehouse
ahead. "Careful now. Take it slow and easy. There'll be
guards posted."

"Right," Rick answered and froze.

From out of nowhere the distinctive cold roundness of
a pistol barrel pressed to the back of the young man's
neck. A deep, masculine voice warned:

"Slow and easy. And don't make any sudden moves—
any of you. There's only three of you and four of us."

How? Rick shivered when the hard steel nudged his
flesh. He was unable to conceive how one man, let alone
four, could have crept up behind them.

"Mark?" Sheryl Lee questioned without turning. "Is
that you?"

"Huh? Sher—" the unseen man stammered. "Sheryl
Lee?"

The redhead turned. "Does it look like anyone else?"

"I thought that . . ." The pressure of the barrel on
Rick's neck lessened.

"I know what you thought, but you were wrong. Put
that pistol down; these are friends of mine. We need to
see my mother *now*," she said before the man could
complete his sentence.

The pistol barrel eased from Rick's neck. The Californian turned around. A tall bear of a man—one man, not
four—stood behind him. The hulking giant stammered
again and cleared his throat before stepping from behind
a bushy shrub that had concealed his bulk in the night.

"Sheryl Lee, Brad's in charge now." Mark's voice was
barely a whisper.

"Brad? Why?" the redhead asked.

"It's your mother, Sheryl Lee. She's . . . she's
dead," Mark managed to say.

"Dead? How?"

Even in the dark Rick saw Sheryl Lee stiffen under the
impact of the stranger's words. He heard her breathing

quicken and the tightness in her voice. He wanted to reach out and touch her, but Charlie stood in the way.

"A couple of nights ago she led a raid on the processing center in the Cotton Bowl," Mark explained. "She was hit by three of the lizards' energy bolts."

"Then we need to see Brad," Sheryl Lee said, her voice quavering as though she was struggling to hold back tears and sorrow.

Mark stepped from the shadows, lifted an arm high, and waved. A guard stepped from behind a hedgerow beside the electronics warehouse and returned the signal.

"It's clear," the bearlike Mark said. "Jace will take you to Brad."

As Sheryl Lee turned, Rick moved to her side and reached out to take her hand. "Sheryl Lee, I . . ."

She pulled from him; her head jerked around to reveal tear-misted eyes. "Not now. I haven't time to mourn her now." She looked away and continued across the street.

"Let her be, son," Charlie whispered while the guard Jace led them inside the warehouse. "She'll handle it in her own way and time. It's a matter of priorities."

Rick sucked in a breath and nodded. The task at hand was for the living. Tears for the dead, even one so loved, must be set aside until there was time for grief.

The Brad Sheryl Lee had asked to see was a lean, balding man in his late thirties who sat behind a littered desk in a small office lit by three candles. He offered his sympathy for the young woman's loss, expressed his own sorrow, then got down to business. "Where's Jo Bob? Who are these two? And most importantly, where in the hell are the medical supplies you were to bring in?"

Slowly, her voice threatening to break with each word, Sheryl Lee answered his questions one after another, ending with a question of her own: "What can you do to clear a way for us into the city?"

The Dallas resistance leader leaned back in his chair and ran a hand through his thinning hair. "The first thing

is you don't bring the pickups into Fort Worth. The
Visitors have been unusually active for the past twenty-
four hours. It's plain to see why. They're expecting you
to make a run in from the west. What you'll do is come
in to Dallas from the south."

"Dallas?" Charlie arched an eyebrow.

"Dallas." Brad tugged open a desk drawer and pulled
out a road map, which he spread over the papers on his
desk. His finger found a dot on the map west of Fort
Worth and traced downward. "You said the trucks are
waiting in Mineral Wells. Then what you'll have to do is
drop south to Stephenville along U.S. 281. From there
swing east on U.S. 67 to Midlothian, then Highway 287
will take you to Interstate 35E."

Rick followed the man's finger while it moved over the
map. What might have been an hour's drive into Fort
Worth grew to at least five hours along an indirect route
that was all open road.

He paused and looked up at the trio. "Once on the
interstate you turn north and it's a straight shot into
Dallas."

"And right up to the Visitor roadblock at the city
limits—that is, if we get that far," Sheryl Lee said.

"I can't help you with gettin' past the roadblock.
You're on your own there. Although with the skyfighter
you have, you'll be carryin' a damn sight more firepower
than we have." Brad paused and rubbed at his head again
before jabbing a finger at the map. "Here's a shoppin'
center just off the interstate a mile past the roadblock. I
can have enough cars and drivers waiting there at, let's
say two in the morning, to unload the medical supplies
from the trucks."

He looked up at Charlie. "That way your friends will
have a shot at startin' back to their homes before the sun
comes up. No need gettin' them stuck in the city. Not
when the whole purpose of our operation here is to
evacuate Dallas."

"They'll appreciate that, friend," Charlie answered.

Brad continued, explaining that once the medical supplies were loaded into the cars the drivers would take their cargo to various locations in Dallas and Fort Worth to be hidden and distributed.

"What about diversions to draw the Visitors' attention away from the roads?" Sheryl Lee pressed. "All this plannin' is no good unless we can get to Dallas with the trucks."

"I was comin' to that," Brad replied. "We have a little surprise planned for the snakes tonight. We're goin' to hit the processin' center up at the old speedway. That should help divert their attention a mite. Other than that, there's not much else we can do."

"Yes, there is." This from Charlie. "That is, if you've got a pilot among your men. There's another skyfighter just sittin' and goin' to waste back on the Brazos. If we could get it in the air, it could be put to good use."

Brad smiled. "Mr. Scoggin, I like the way you think. Jace, the man who brought you in, used to be stationed at Carswell over in Fort Worth. He flew B-52s. Will he do?"

Charlie nodded. "He'll need a tailgunner with him."

"Mark's a hell of a shot," Brad replied. "Anything else?"

"Yes," Rick finally said. "I thought this area and the land to the west was beyond the Visitors' safe zone. Yet there're snakes crawling all over the place. What's going on? Have they developed an immunity to the red dust?"

Brad shook his head. "It had me fooled for a while too. This is Texas, friend. The summer's are long, hot, and dry. This summer and fall we've had a double dose of all three. The bacteria hasn't had the cold spell it needs to regenerate. 'Til a blue norther blows in from the Arctic, just about all of Texas is a safe zone for the snakes."

"This is no time to be discussin' the weather." Sheryl Lee glanced at Rick. "We need to move if we intend to make our two o'clock appointment."

Brad stood and let his gaze drift over the faces of the three standing before his desk. "I don't need to tell you how much those supplies are needed here. And I don't need to tell you to be careful. All I can do is offer a wish for the best of luck."

He took and shook each of their hands before they turned and left the cramped, candle-lit office. A few minutes later four men and one woman wove their way through the night back to the waiting station wagon.

Chapter 18

Mark pushed from the cedar break, arms piled high with Visitor uniforms and helmets. Sheryl Lee and Rick watched while the man walked to where they stood and carefully deposited the burden at their feet.

"Four of 'em are usable," the bear of a man grunted. "The others were pretty messy. Sheryl Lee, I wish your friends had been carryin' something other than shotguns. Snake uniforms are damned hard to come by. I hate to see four blown to hell like that."

Rick swallowed any reply to the Dallasite's grisly comments. Stripping dead Visitors wasn't his idea of how to spend the evening. But running a convoy of drug-laden pickup trucks halfway across Texas straight into a Visitor roadblock wasn't either.

Nor did the Californian question what purpose Mark had for the alien uniforms. As the man said, Visitor uniforms were hard to come by, and in a city overrun by lizards they would be put to good use.

"Wish Brad and the others had these," Mark continued with a sad shake of his head. "Might make gettin' close to the processin' center a bit easier tonight."

"And I wish Charlie and Jace would get back," Sheryl Lee answered impatiently. "How long have they been gone?"

Rick checked his wristwatch. "Twenty minutes. Not long, to teach a man the controls of an unfamiliar aircraft."

"It's twenty minutes we could have been on the road," the redhead snapped. "It's a long way to Dallas, and we have a two o'clock appointment to keep."

Rick ignored the razor sharpness of her tongue. She had more than ample reason to be on edge.

"Here they come." Mark pointed to a pale white form that slid beneath a waning moon toward the small clearing.

Rick watched the alien vessel as it shot over the tops of the stunted oaks and cedars. It wobbled from side to side, but was far less erratic than the first flight he had taken with Charlie a few hours ago. The ship slowed, stopped in midair above the sandy clearing, then gently sank to the ground beside the second ship squatted on the ground. The craft's side door opened, its halves swinging up and down.

"So much for formal instruction," Charlie said when he stepped from the skyfighter. "Jace has just moved into the earn-while-you-learn phase of his flyin' career. Anything else about this baby, he'll have to pick up while in the air."

Jace exited the craft just behind the older man. "She's enough like our own aircraft. I can handle her."

"Now if you two are through pattin' yourselves on the back, can we get the hell out of here?" Sheryl Lee nudged Rick aside and strode toward the nearest sky-fighter. "We have six trucks to get into Dallas."

Charlie's head swiveled toward Rick. The older man arched a questioning eyebrow. The Californian shook his head, indicating that the pilot should let the young woman's irritation pass. Charlie pursed his lips and nodded.

"You heard the li'l' lady, boys," Charlie said. "Let's get this show on the road!"

Gathering uniforms and helmets from the ground, Mark hastened into a ship with Jace, while Rick and Charlie entered the second craft. They found Sheryl Lee waiting in the co-pilot's seat, staring out the ship's window. Without a word the two men took their seats fore and aft. Seconds later, Charlie lifted into the air and banked the skyfighter toward Mineral Wells.

Silence hung heavy in the ship's cramped interior. Like a statue, Sheryl Lee rigidly sat in her seat, her gaze never leaving the night outside. On the flight from Dallas, both men had tried to talk with her, tried to console her, and received icy glares in return. Now they allowed her to cope with her grief in her own way, although Rick worried that she wasn't handling it at all but only letting it gnaw at her. In spite of the task at hand, her reaction wasn't normal.

It was *her mother who was killed!* Rick sensed the pressure that built in his companion as he studied her taut profile in the ship's dim interior lights. *There should be tears. She has to release some of what she's holding back before she explodes*.

When that explosion might occur tripled his worries. Tonight of all nights Sheryl Lee needed to be in total control of her senses and emotions. One slipup, no matter how small, could endanger the caravan and the precious cargo it carried—not to mention the lives of the men and women who had volunteered for the hazardous journey.

The skyfighter's engines whined down. Rick glanced out the craft's window to see Jace nearly overshoot them before he managed to slow the ship he piloted. Together the alien vehicles floated down to the junkyard.

Only when Charlie opened the door to his ship and called out did the others reveal their hiding places. One by one six motors rumbled to life among the shells of wrecked cars and trucks. The pickups trundled before the skyfighters, their doors opening and the men and women inside stepping out.

"Folks, we've had a minor change in our plans for

tonight," Charlie began, and quickly outlined the planned route for the run.

Here and there Rick heard a few mumbles, but no one openly questioned the route. When Charlie finished, the survivors of the cross-Texas trek turned back to their trucks.

"I'm goin' with them." Sheryl Lee appeared beside Rick at the exit of the skyfighter.

Reaching out, the Californian grasped her shoulder. "You can't. You're supposed to remain with us."

"Don't tell me what I can and can't do, Surfer Boy." She pivoted and stood facing him. "Those supplies out there are mine, not yours. I've brought them this far, and I intend to ride with them all the way into Dallas. Hell, you wouldn't even be here if Joe Bob hadn't saved your backside in Los Angeles."

Rick stared at her, uncertain what to say. The sudden savage verbal attack took him completely off guard. "But I thought it was understood you were to ride with Charlie and me?"

"You *mis*understood. I'm staying with those supplies. And that is all there is to it. Understand that?" She turned again to leave the ship.

Rick reached for her again; Charlie's arm interceded.

"Let her go, son," the older man said. "She'll be just as safe with the trucks as she would be in here with us. Maybe safer."

Rick watched the redhead climb into the convoy's lead pickup and slam the door after her. He glanced at Charlie and sucked at his teeth in disgust. "I don't like it."

"At the moment I don't think she gives a damn what either of us likes or doesn't like." He tilted his head to the tailgunner's seat. "Come on, we've got a long night ahead of us, and it ain't gettin' any shorter with us standin' here."

*   *   *

Nothing. Garth listened to the reports of the recalled ships. The search had been a waste! For a whole day he had disrupted normal processing traffic from both Fort Worth and Abilene and had nothing to show for it. *The bitch's offspring is as cunning as her mother!*

The Houston Mother Ship commander rubbed at the corners of his eyes in an attempt to relieve the irritation of his human-imitating lenses. It didn't help. He needed to remove them and give his eyes an opportunity to breathe.

"All the Abilene ships have returned to base," Major Lawrence said from Garth's right. "As soon as their crews are relieved, they will resume transporting captured humans to the Abilene Processing Center."

Garth nodded, suppressing the urge to order the ships to resume the search. He couldn't afford to divert men and equipment from their assigned duties any longer. The processing centers would have to work double shifts around the clock for the next week to make up for today's delay.

He grimaced. Only last night he had allowed himself a moment of pride in the dramatic increase in his command's production rate. Tonight he faced the realization that with the destruction of the two centers in Dallas and Fort Worth as well as the time spent in his search, he would be hard pressed to meet this month's quota.

My search, he tried to reprimand himself for the wasteful expenditure of his troops' energy. He couldn't. The human female meant too much to him; she would bear him a star child. There was more than simple revenge for a lost hand at the root of his actions. With a star child at his command, Earth would be his—for the greater glory of the Leader, of course.

Where could she have hidden? The question that had haunted him all day refused to be pushed from his mind. A woman and an airplane load of medical supplies just didn't vanish into thin air. Of that he was certain.

And they hadn't. Reports from searchers early that morning told of deep automobile-tire tracks cut through wheat fields seventy-five miles east of where the wrecked transport plane had been brought down. The woman had found someone to aid her in transporting the medical supplies into the Dallas–Fort Worth area. Of that he was almost certain. There was no other logical conclusion that fit the facts.

And she's on her way here to Fort Worth. She has to be, he told himself with less conviction than he had felt that morning. *There is nowhere else for her to go.*

Yet, where was she now? Had she and her cohorts continued on a westward path, they would have reached Fort Worth by now. And there was no way into the city except through his roadblocks.

"Commander," Major Lawrence's voice wedged into his thoughts, "two of our Fort Worth skyfighters haven't reported in."

"What?" Garth's eyes narrowed when he turned to his fellow officer.

"Two skyfighters assigned to search the Mineral Wells sector have not reported in," Lawrence said. He paused to clear his throat. "The last communiqué from them was four hours ago."

"Four hours?" Garth stiffened. "Four hours have passed without hearing from two ships, and you've just received word of this? It was my assumption that you were in command here, Major."

"Commander, my crews have attempted to coordinate an aerial search of three hundred ships today. That two skyfighters somehow—"

"Major!" A sergeant seated at the communications console swiveled around in his chair. "I think you'd better listen to this! We've got a resistance assault on our blockade across Interstate 20."

"Put it on the loudspeaker," Major Lawrence ordered.

The sergeant flicked a switch. A panicked voice

crackled from a speaker hung near the ceiling of the room.

". . . twenty . . . maybe thirty in all. Coming at us from both sides. We can hold for another five or ten minutes. Then we have to have reinforcements. . . ."

Garth's gaze darted to a map of Fort Worth pinned on a wall beside him. Interstate 20 was the major artery into the city from the west. This was it! The resistance was opening a way to bring the medical supplies into the city!

"Major, I want two hundred shock troopers sent to the roadblock immediately!" Garth's pulse raced. "The woman we've been looking for is about to play right into my hands!"

Chapter 19

Rick shifted his weight in the seat, but the movement did nothing to relieve the nagging ache in his lower back. The long hours of inactivity were slowly taking their toll.

Better than long hours of activity, he told himself while he checked the display screen before him. As for the past four hours, it showed the same thing—one single blip, Jace's ship, which flew a parallel course fifty yards to the right. Why or how they and the convoy had escaped detection for five hours of traveling over open roads he didn't know. He just thanked whatever powers guided their fates.

His attention turned to the line of pickup trucks on the deserted highway below. Like a segmented serpent, they followed the skyfighters' searchlight in a tight line. Except for having to weave a path around abandoned cars in the streets of Stephenville and Midlothian, the drive had gone without a hitch. He smiled. In fact, the trucks had managed to maintain the once-legal speed limit of fifty-five miles an hour.

The searchlights revealed rolling farmland and occasional clumps of trees to each side of the road. Even in the harsh bluish light, Rick detected lush greens covering the land. The browns and reds of West Texas sand and stone were behind them now, Charlie had explained, saying they had entered north central Texas, where rainfall was abundant.

Shifting his weight again, Rick allowed himself a moment of self-satisfaction. Using the searchlights had been his idea. The two skyfighters flew on opposite sides of the highway ahead of the caravan, their searchlights bathing the ground beneath them. To an alien observer, the ships would appear to be scouring the road, a perfect ruse when all the Visitor forces seemed to be out looking for them. However, the searchlights provided illumination for the convoy, which accounted for the trucks' brisk speed.

"Resistance attack reported on Arlington headquarters," a static-crackling voice came from the speaker grille at the front of the alien ship. "Units Forty and Forty-One, you are to reroute from the Hurst fire. Proceed immediately to Arlington headquarters and there provide aerial support. Units Nineteen and Thirty-Six, secure your location and proceed to Arlington headquarters."

"Hot damn! Will you listen to that?" Charlie's laughter roared through the small craft. "That Brad and his crew have had the snakes jumpin' all night!"

Rick grinned. Charlie did not exaggerate, although he omitted the Fort Worth resistance's participation in the constant harassment of the Visitors they had monitored on the ship's radio. At least twelve times since the convoy began its journey to Dallas, the lizards had reported attacks within the two cities.

To be certain, none of the assaults were major or long-lived. A group in Fort Worth began the series of attacks with a quick attack on a roadblock in the western part of the city. Their gunshots had lasted just long enough for two hundred shock troopers to be sent to the area. Fifteen minutes later snipers opened fire on a ground patrol in south Dallas. Firebombs tossed into a shock trooper garrison in the suburb of Irving, burning tires rolled into a landing squad vehicle in north Fort Worth—again and again the resistance forces struck. Each incident sent Visitor troops scurrying to another portion of the cities.

"Brad's softening them up, confusing them before he hits the processing center," Rick called forward to Charlie. "By the time the real attack comes, they'll think it's just another brushfire."

Charlie's laughter continued. "He's going to make it a mite easier on us when we hit the roadblock. The snakes'll be so scattered out they won't know whether to scratch their heads or their scaly tails!"

With luck, that was just the way it would be. Or so Rick hoped. Even with the support of two skyfighters, those on the ground were going to need all the help they could get.

Rick lifted his right arm and squinted at the face of his watch—one-thirty. The caravan had thirty minutes until the rendezvous with the fleet of cars Brad had promised.

"Waxahachie city limits dead ahead," Charlie said. "We're runnin' right on schedule. Twenty-one more miles and we've pulled it off."

Rick watched the caravan turn onto Interstate 35E. Still driving without headlights, they moved northward on the last leg of their journey.

"Nineteen miles," Charlie counted down the distance remaining between the trucks and the Visitor roadblock ahead.

When he reached ten, the skyfighter's engines whined in a high-pitched scream. Charlie, with Jace keeping pace, pushed the small craft forward through the night. Both ships directed their searchlights dead ahead, then switched them off.

"I can see their lights. Target's right in front of our nose!" Charlie called back to his tailgunner. "Here we go!"

Rick felt the skyfighter nose downward. When it leveled, the highway's surface was a mere ten feet below the ship's rear window. His thumbs arched over the tops of the seat's gun grips to lightly rest on the red buttons there.

"Searchlights—on!" Charlie thumbed the glaring beams back on, their harsh light meant to momentarily blind the Visitor guards who manned the roadblock. "Now to give them a taste of their own medicine."

Even over the skyfighter's engines, Rick heard the sizzling hiss of energy bolts as Charlie unleashed the ship's nose cannons on the unsuspecting alien roadblock.

"Give 'em everything you've got, son!" Charlie called out.

At the same time the ship nosed upward to avoid colliding with the Visitors' barricade. Rick's thumbs depressed the firing buttons. A trail of blue-white energy globes burst from the twin tailguns, strafing the scattering shock troopers as the craft shot over the roadblock. A similar line of bolts came from Jace's ship when Mark opened up with his own barrage.

A shower of flames leaped into the air as the deadly light beams struck home. The wooden barricade exploded, clearing a path for the trucks that barreled up the highway.

"That did it!" Rick shouted. "We opened the way!"

"No harm in givin' the snakes another run, is there?" Charlie answered.

The skyfighter banked to the left in a 180-degree turn and nosed back toward the ground. Again the sizzle of Charlie's nose cannons came from the front of the ship.

Rick heard the radio come alive again, this time with a panicked report of their aerial assault. The cry for help went unanswered. Another alarm drowned that of the shock troopers below—an officer reported an allout attack on Dallas' remaining processing center.

The instant Rick felt the older man pull the ship skyward, he pressed the firing buttons and held them down. This time, however, he directed the two guns in wide, sweeping arcs, spraying energy blasts into the

fleeing shock troopers on each side of the road. Two,
maybe three of the alien warriors fell beneath the searing
barrage. Rick couldn't be certain because Charlie banked
the ship in another tight turn.

"This is it, son. All or nothin'."

When the Korean War veteran leveled the craft, they
once more flew over the convoy of pickup trucks.
Maneuvering the skyfighter ahead of the lead truck,
Charlie eased the ship to within ten feet of the pavement
again. His nose cannons blasted fiery death for a third
time.

Rick jerked his hands away from the firing grips when
the ship lurched up into the night sky. He didn't dare risk
firing with the pickups right behind them. They hadn't
come across Texas to be taken out by friendly fire.

Below, four trucks raced through the wide hole in the
Visitor barricade before the still-living shock troopers
realized what was happening. The last two trucks sped
through the gap while the Visitors lifted weapons and
fired wild shots after the disappearing vehicles.

"Slick as hell," Charlie chuckled while he surveyed
the scene below. "Jace can keep 'em pinned down for a
while now. We've other matters to attend to."

The blue glow faded from Rick's window as Charlie
switched off the skyfighter's searchlight. To the left the
Californian saw Jace wing his ship in a tight arc and
circle back on the shock troopers beside the highway. His
forward cannons, then Mark's rear guns erupted when
the craft swooped over the still-flaming remains of the
roadblock.

The pickup convoy appeared beneath the window. One
by one the craft passed over the six trucks until it once
more flew at the head of the line.

"There's the shoppin' center ahead, and the turnoff,"
Charlie announced. "And the cars Brad promised!"

His gaze moving between the display screen and
window, Rick watched as the skyfighter rose five

hundred feet over the shopping center to hover above the waiting cars. The searchlight came back on, flooding the parking lot with artificial sunlight. Like ants scurrying between toy cars, the resistance fighters hurried from their vehicles to meet the incoming trucks and the boxes packed on their beds.

Ten minutes passed before the last car was loaded and drove into the night with Sheryl Lee sitting in its passenger seat. Below, the farmers and ranchers who had survived the treacherous journey, many of whom were still nameless to Rick, looked up and waved their arms before climbing back into their vehicles.

"Time to get the folks started on their way home," Charlie said from the pilot's seat.

The skyfighter swung about to begin the flight south. The voice on the Visitors' radio returned.

With fingers pressed to pounding temples, Garth listened to the reports flooding Fort Worth Processing Center Two from the North Dallas installation. From the first alarm of the resistance's attack, the communiqués had grown more bleak. Now there was nothing. The last message had ended in an explosive burst of static. Garth needed no official report to tell him the obvious—the last Dallas processing center had fallen and lay in smoldering ruins.

"Commander," Major Lawrence said from Garth's left. "Five squad vehicles with two hundred shock troopers will arrive at the North Dallas facility in five minutes."

Five minutes! A dry, humorless chuckle pushed from Garth's throat. Five minutes might as well have been an eternity. By the time the reinforcements landed, the enemy would be gone, vanished back into the night that had spawned it.

"Where does their ingenuity come from, Major?" Garth asked without turning to the officer.

"Ingenuity, Commander? Certainly you don't mean the murderous rabble out there!" Indignation showed in Lawrence's words. "They are nothing more than animals—stupid animals!"

"Animals, yes, but very resourceful animals, Major." Garth shook his head. Was the major blind to what had occurred tonight? "Can't you see the pattern?"

Major Lawrence did not reply.

"The attacks, Major, the scattered hit-and-run attacks throughout both cities tonight!" Garth continued. "They were but a ruse designed to disorient us, to leave us off balance. When we reeled, our troops spread too thin, they struck their primary target. It's so clear now with the blessing of hindsight."

"You read too much into tonight's action, Commander," Lawrence answered. "What we have here is what we have always faced in this sector—random acts of violence by mindless creatures! There is no pattern, only cattle who struggle against their master's yoke."

Garth sat silently. The major *was* a fool. When Garth returned to Houston he would have the man recalled to the Mother Ship. There was always need of individuals gifted with Lawrence's extraordinary insight to clean the ship's septic tanks.

"Major," the sergeant at the communications console called over a shoulder. "It's the roadblock on Interstate 35E again."

Lawrence waved the man away, but Garth sat straight in his chair. He had forgotten about the Dallas roadblock during the assault on the processing center.

"Put it on the loudspeaker, Sergeant," Garth ordered.

The man flicked a switch, and a quavering voice echoed within the room. In short, quick gasps the voice described two skyfighters attacking the blockade and several trucks that ran the roadblock.

With each word another horrible piece fell into place. Garth grimaced; the pattern of the attacks expanded. The destruction of the processing center had not been the human resistance fighters' primary objective. It had been yet another diversion. One that had allowed them to bring the medical supplies into Dallas—and with those supplies the woman he searched for!

His pulse raced. Even as he sat here, the resistance was transporting the supplies through Dallas, and perhaps Fort Worth!

"Major, I want every available squad vehicle and skyfighter at your command in the air!" Garth swiveled around in his chair to explain the scene he visualized. "I want them captured, Major. Captured, not killed."

Chapter 20

Jace took the lead as the two skyfighters swung about in a tight 180-degree turn and headed north toward Dallas. Shadows moving in the night, Rick glimpsed the six trucks as they wheeled from the interstate and rolled westward.

"Why don't you come up front here and keep me company?" Charlie glanced over his shoulder. "I think things have quieted down a bit."

A tap of the black button on the left side of the gunner's seat and the minidisplay retracted into the chair's arm. Rick pushed to his feet and stretched, his palms brushing the craft's ceiling. The joints in his arms and legs popped.

Charlie chuckled while the Californian walked forward and sank into the co-pilot's seat. "You sound as old as I look."

"Which is about a hundred years younger than I feel," Rick answered. His gaze turned to the approaching city outside.

"When we get our feet back on the ground, we'll find us two rockin' chairs and sit around and listen to our bones creak." Charlie looked at his young friend and grinned.

Ahead Jace's ship banked a few degrees to the west. Charlie imitated the maneuver.

"You have to admit that it went easier than any of us expected," Charlie said while he leveled the skyfighter.

"Yes, I do have to admit that. Although I wouldn't want to make a daily routine of tonight's activities." Rick nodded.

Lights blinked alive at the periphery of his vision. His head jerked to the right. Three more lights appeared in the sky to the east.

"Charlie, what the hell is that?" As he spoke, additional lights flashed on ahead.

"Damned if it doesn't look like Visitor ships switching on their searchlights." The older man's brow furrowed with deep creases. "They're flyin' mighty low."

The beams of light *were* from alien vessels. Rick watched the searchlights sweep across the ground.

"They're after something—Brad and the others who hit the processing center or . . ." Charlie grunted.

Rick didn't want to consider the unspoken "or" Charlie had repressed. Nor could he edge the thought away. Sheryl Lee was down there. The snakes might be searching for the cars and the medical supplies.

"Best make it appear that we're doing the same thing."

Charlie's right hand lifted to the control console, tapping a button to glowing white life. The searchlight beamed down from the belly of the skyfighter, illuminating block on block of homes in a look-alike housing development.

"Now to bring her down a mite." He nosed the craft closer to the tops of the trees.

Ahead of them Jace's searchlight beamed on and his ship slid down until it matched Charlie's altitude.

"They're not interested in us," Rick said, watching the other aerial lights that moved over Dallas. "Wonder what's going on? We haven't heard anything over the radio for the past fifteen minutes."

Charlie shook his head and eased the ship closer to the ground as Jace led them over a narrow, winding ribbon of black. Rick recognized the Trinity River from their evening flight above Dallas yesterday.

"Looks like he's taking us back to the warehouse district." Rick saw Jace's ship drop even lower after the two craft shot above the rubble that marked what had once been Dallas' downtown.

"So it seems." Charlie edged the ship down after Jace until the skyfighters skimmed over a wide road lined with warehouses on each side. "He's slowing."

Jace did, then stopped. The ship's searchlight blinking once before flashing off. Charlie killed his own searchlight. A wink of a flashlight came from a warehouse on the west side of the street. As Rick turned to find its source, he saw one of the warehouse's great doors slide upward.

Immediately, Jace's ship swung around to face the opening, then floated toward the gaping darkness with Charlie right on his tail. The rattle of the door closing behind them vibrated through the ship as Charlie gently let the craft settle to the ground. Lights flared overhead.

"What the hell!" Rick blinked, trying to focus.

"I'll be damned." Charlie whistled. "I've got to get a better look at this."

He opened the skyfighter's door, pushed from the seat, and strode from the ship. The Californian, still half blinded by the lights, stumbled after the Korean War veteran.

"Welcome to Little Love," Jace greeted the two as they stared at the warehouse's interior. "We named it after Dallas' Love Field."

Rick stared in disbelief. The warehouse had been converted into an airplane hangar that contained a single-engine plane and a helicopter. Two-man work crews busied themselves about the aircraft.

"That Piper Cub looks brand spankin' new." Charlie whistled in admiration. "Somebody's put a lot of work into her."

Jace nodded. "She's mine. My father taught me to fly in her. Used to have another copter, but the snakes shot it down about a month back."

"How do you get them out of here?" This from Rick. "How do you take off?"

"No problem with the copter. Just push it outside and lift off," Jace replied while Mark and he escorted them to a side door. "As for the Cub, we just came in on Little Love's one and only runway—the street outside."

Jace waved an arm, and the warehouse lights went off. The door opened and the pilot stepped outside. "We're three blocks from headquarters. Brad'll be waiting to hear from us."

Without another word the four slipped through the shadows toward Dallas resistance headquarters.

"Somethin's up." Charlie nudged Rick's shoulder and tilted his head toward the opposite side of the warehouse the Dallas resistance called headquarters.

Rick lowered the plastic cup of coffee he nursed. Two men carrying deer rifles stationed themselves beside a door. With glances at each other, they swung the door open and stepped into the night, slamming the door behind them.

"The sentries have spotted someone or something," Mark explained in an even voice. "It happens around three or four times a night. Just enough to keep everybody edgy. Ninety percent of the time it's nothin' more than a stray cat or dog."

"The other ten percent?" Rick questioned.

"Let's just say the snakes haven't located this place for three months," Mark replied as he took a sip from his cup of coffee. "We don't let anyone get close enough to get a good look."

The door the men had disappeared through flew open. The two returned, dragging a third man between them as they crossed into Brad's office.

"That looked like Buster." Jace's eyes shifted to Mark. "Wasn't he drivin' one of the cars tonight?"

Mark thought a moment and nodded. "Looked like he was in pretty bad shape."

Brad stepped from his office and called, "Charlie, Rick, I think you two should hear this."

Coffee in hand, the two rose and walked into the resistance leader's office. The man Jace and Mark had identified as Buster sat slumped in a chair. He pressed a crimson-stained handkerchief to a nasty-looking gash on his forehead.

"He was in the car with Sheryl Lee," Brad whispered. "They ran into Visitors."

"A whole damned squad of 'em," Buster spat. "We hadn't driven more than a mile from the shopping center when we ran head-on into a ground patrol."

The injured man detailed the high-speed flight he and his passenger had made in an attempt to lose the Visitor shock troopers. He estimated the chase lasted only another mile when a second ground patrol appeared.

"We wheeled onto a residential street and plowed into an overturned van. That's when I cracked my head against the windshield." Buster winced painfully as he shifted in the chair. "Sheryl Lee was thrown from the car. I'm not certain exactly what happened then."

He said that he managed to stumble from the wreck and around the car to aid the redhead. She was gone.

"She was runnin' directly toward the snakes," he said. "I called after her. She didn't stop. Dazed, confused, hurt—I don't know, but she didn't stop. She just kept runnin' . . . just kept runnin'. Right into the lizards' hands!"

An ice floe moved through Rick's veins. Sheryl Lee was a captive of the Visitors! After all she had endured and survived to bring the medical supplies into Dallas, she had reached her destination only to be trapped by an overturned van lying in the middle of a street.

Buster's head lowered, and he sobbed. "I couldn't do a thing to help her. I was only one man against all those slimy bastards. So I ran. God help me, I left her with *them*—those damned *things*—and I ran."

Brad sympathetically squeezed the man's shoulder. "There was nothin' you or anyone else could have done. You can't blame yourself for what happened. Like you said, she was dazed and confused. She didn't know what she was doin'."

Buster sadly shook his head and mumbled an account of his flight from the ground patrols and the hot-wiring of a car to escape the Visitors.

Rick barely heard him. His thoughts centered on Sheryl Lee and the fate that awaited his angel in khaki at the hands of the alien invaders. It couldn't end for her like this. The redhead was too full of life, too determined, too strong to . . .

He lied to himself. It would end exactly like it had ended for millions of men, women, and children who had been brimming with life when the Visitors captured them. Sheryl Lee would die or be transformed into a reptilian frozen dinner. *Unless we do something.*

"Where would they take her?" Rick looked up at his companions.

Brad's gaze lifted to the Californian. "If she's still alive, I'd guess to a local transport center and then on to the processin' center in Fort Worth, the one at Carswell. It's the only one left standin' in the area."

"Still alive?" Rick's voice rose. "Is there any reason to think she's not alive?"

"No." Brad rubbed at his balding head. "But she could have been hurt in the accident. There's no way to be certain."

"She wasn't hurt!" He refused to accept that the young woman was dead. "Confused, yes, but injured . . . well, maybe. She was running, Brad. She ran. A seriously wounded person can't run!"

"Which means she's being transported to Fort Worth," the Dallas resistance leader replied. "That's the same as being dead."

"What?" Rick couldn't believe what he heard. "How can you say that?"

"Son, what else can he say?" This from Charlie, who turned a drawn and tired face to the younger man.

"He can say that we're going in and get her!" Rick shouted, unable to contain his mounting frustration and anger. "Sheryl Lee deserves that much! She's alive and that means there's a chance of getting her out."

Brad stiffened. "Get her out? How? What do you suggest we do—drive up to the processin' center's gate and tell the snakes we've come for Sheryl Lee Darcy? Because that's about all we can do right now. Ninety percent of my forces are scattered across Dallas tonight. We hit a processin' center, remember? They're hidin' because the snakes are swarmin' the city searchin' for them. Hell, I'd be lucky if I could raise twenty men and women for your little suicide mission."

"Twenty men and women can do a hell of a lot." Rick stood his ground.

"Rick, it's no good," Jace said. "What happened to Sheryl Lee is what could happen to any of us. We all know that and accept the risk. It's not pretty, but that's what we have to live with."

"Twenty people stormin' a processin' center." Brad snorted and rolled his eyes. "It's true, it's really true. All you Californians are *loco*!"

It was crazy, and Rick knew it. But he couldn't let the Visitors take Sheryl Lee, not without fighting. "Then I'll go after her myself."

His companions sighed in disgust and shook their heads. It was Mark who spoke. "Now you *are* talkin' crazy. Why don't you just take that energy pistol you're carryin' and put it to your head? It'd be quicker."

Energy pistol? Rick glanced at the weapon stuffed under his belt. The seed of an idea took root. His mind raced, trying to jam pieces to a puzzle together as he went.

"There're the Visitors uniforms in the skyfighters." He glared at the bear of a man. "With this pistol and a uniform, I might, just might be able to get into the center."

"Not much chance they'd let you through the gate," Brad replied.

"Then I'll fly in. I've watched Charlie work the skyfighter's controls. I can't guarantee I'll make it, but, dammit, it's worth a try!" Rick would not be denied.

"There'll be no need of you doin' that." Charlie sat up. " 'Cause I'll be pilotin' you. I'm sure I can wiggle into one of those uniforms."

"Brad, he's onto something." Jace turned to the resistance leader. "The snakes aren't goin' to question skyfighters landin' at the processin' center, especially if those ships are haulin' prisoners. Say, twenty prisoners."

"All with weapons tucked under their shirts." A humorless smile spread across Mark's face. "Four shock trooper guards and twenty prisoners—we'd have a shot at pullin' it off, Brad."

Brad's head moved from side to side as he sank into the chair behind his littered desk. He sucked in a hissing breath. "It wouldn't work. Twenty-four people aren't enough to go up against the guards in that processin' center. It would still be suicide."

He paused to draw another deep breath. "However, if those twenty-four were to get a little outside help, just enough to create a diversion, then . . ." His voice trailed off, and he smiled.

"You've got a plan, don't you, cowboy?" Jace raised his eyebrows at his friend.

"I just might. It'll be risky and it depends on the situation in Fort Worth, but," Brad glanced at Rick, "it's Sheryl Lee we're talkin' about here. And she deserves that much from us. Now all of you get the hell out of my office. I've got to try and raise Fort Worth on the radio."

Chapter 21

Doubts assailed Rick's mind as Charlie switched on the skyfighter and guided the craft from the resistance's warehouse hangar. What had seemed so clear and simple in Brad's office was now clouded and cut through with a thousand ifs.

To begin with, the stolen uniform he wore was at least two sizes too large for him; it fit like a floppy tent. And the helmet about his head felt like an ill-balanced melon. Then there was the face mask. With that dark sheet of plastic dropped before his eyes, he could barely see inches in front of him, or at least it seemed that way. He knew the Visitors were sensitive to the sun's light, but he had never realized they were *this* sensitive. Their home world must be in a continous state of semidarkness, he mused.

He glanced over a shoulder to watch Jace's ship exit the hangar, but couldn't see a thing. The ten resistance volunteers who had packed themselves into the small craft completely blocked his view of the skyfighter's aft window.

At least they look the part. Rick perused the faces of the ten men and women. *They look like drugged zombies being led to the slaughter.*

It wasn't a drug that brought the dazed expressions to their faces, he recognized. It was fear, simple cold fear. The fact that each carried a weapon concealed in his or her clothing—a pistol, .45 caliber at the minimum, or an

Uzi or a sawed-off shotgun if they wore a coat or jacket to hide the bulk—did absolutely nothing to ease that gnawing fear.

Every one of them was fully aware of the fact that they were entering the dragon's den. This den swarmed with at least two hundred reptiles, each armed with pulse-beam energy-spitting pistols and rifles.

"Time to get this show on the road, Surfer Boy."

Charlie's use of the nickname Sheryl Lee had given him turned Rick's head around. Outside he saw Jace's skyfighter slide beside theirs. In helicopter-imitating fashion, the two ships rose straight in the air, banked west, and shot toward Fort Worth thirty-five miles away.

"Now all we have to do is get inside the Carswell processin' center, find Sheryl Lee—if the snakes have taken her there—then get ourselves back out again in one piece," Brad said from behind Rick's seat.

The Visitor-disguised Californian ignored the resistance leader's less than reassuring tone. The plan of attack was relatively uncomplicated. *If one considers coordinating the activities of two cities' resistance forces uncomplicated*, Rick admitted, realizing the complexity of the dual assault on the processing center.

Phase one hinged on their two Trojan horse skyfighters penetrating Visitor security surrounding the center. If they made it inside—and that was no small if—Fort Worth resistance had agreed to provide the diversion Brad had mentioned in his office. At five o'clock in the morning, four hundred resistance fighters would storm the processing center fully intent on taking and destroying the facility.

During that attack, the Dallas group would free Sheryl Lee while disrupting Visitor defenses from the inside.

"Take a gander at that!" Charlie whistled and pointed ahead. "We still must be twenty miles from the center."

Rick sucked in a deep breath. He didn't need Charlie's finger to locate the lights on the horizon. Like a portion of day blossoming in the night, the processing center sat on the horizon illuminated by searchlights and flood-lights the Visitors had strung about its perimeter. The young man swallowed. Making it through that circular corridor of light would be hell for the Fort Worth force.

Static popped from the control-panel speaker. Rick jumped.

"You're on a heading that will take you directly over Fort Worth Processing Center Two." Rick discerned a voice within the crackling static when he could finally hear above the pounding of his heart. "Please identify yourself and your purpose."

Without blinking an eye, Charlie tapped a white button beside the speaker. "This is . . ." A static-mimicking hiss sputtered from his lips to make it sound as though interference garbled his transmission. "We have twenty prisoners and request permission to land and unload these smelly animals."

A chill raced up and down Rick's spine. The older man pushed it too far with the "smelly animals" comment.

"Please repeat," the voice requested. "I lost half of that in static."

"This is units . . ." Charlie hissed again, louder," . . . from Dallas with . . ." more hissing, . . . prisoners. We request permission to land and unload." He finished with another burst of hissing.

The speaker was silent, as though the Visitor on the opposite end was considering exactly how to handle the situation. Static popped again and the voice returned. "Permission granted. However, you and your co-pilot will be required to maintain guard over your prisoners until they have completed processing."

"What? Our duty was supposed to be over at . . ." Charlie hissed once again. "What's going on down there?"

"I'd lower your voice if I were you," the speaker

answered. "We've got brass up to our hindquarters down here, and they're just looking for heads to roll."

"Understand, Fort Worth," Charlie replied. "What's the problem?"

"Everything," the voice in the speaker answered. "Easiest way to proceed is to 'yes, sir' it and protect your own tail."

"Understood," Charlie said. "And thanks for the advice, Fort Worth. Units . . ." he hissed once more, ". . . out."

Charlie's grin split his narrow face when he punched off the radio and glanced at Rick. "Some things never change. The old radio-static trick! Picked that up in Korea, and it still works like a charm. Used to drive our wing leader crazy!"

Rick released a nervous sigh of relief, but Brad spoke from behind him. "For one, this smelly animal would like to know more about the Visitor brass that were mentioned."

Charlie shrugged. "I did the best I could. Our friend on the radio probably had some of that brass breathin' down his neck."

Rick's attention returned to the skyfighter's window and the processing center's lights. They glowed only five miles away now, and the situation looked far worse than it had appeared from over Dallas. The floodlights illuminated a circle around the center at least a quarter of a mile wide. It would be impossible for anyone to move within that area without being seen.

"Do you think your Fort Worth friends will be able to get through that?" Rick turned to Brad.

"They'll give it all they've got." Brad's eyes widened when they shifted to the front of the skyfighter. "My Lord, what's goin' on down there? It looks like a cattle yard!"

Rick swiveled around. Outside, the processing center loomed below. The reason for the shock that rattled the resistance leader was more than obvious. People were packed behind the center's chain-link perimeter fence like steers crammed into a holding pen. Here and there a sprinkling of red marked the shock trooper guards who herded the human steers.

"It looks like they're running at overload down there." Disgust seeped into Brad's every syllable. "We hurt 'em bad tonight, and they're tryin' to make up for it here. There must be three thousand people waitin' processing."

From the milling mass under guard outside the center, Rick followed a long, serpentinely twisting line of drugged men and women who shuffled one by one into the building. Conveyer belts ran from the back of the center where squad vehicles squatted, ready to be packed with the milky capsules that rode those belts. The Californian's stomach lurched at the thought of the contents stored in each of the capsules.

"I'm takin' us down." Charlie maneuvered the sky-fighter over the rows of waiting shuttles and began to drift earthward near the gate of the massive holding pen.

Rick checked his wristwatch—four-thirty. A half hour remained until the Fort Worth resistance staged their assault.

"And remember we're supposed to be drugged," Brad said to the others in the skyfighter. "That means act drugged. Look dazed, and for the love of God, don't react to anything that's happenin' around you."

A slight vibration ran through the alien craft when it touched the old runway. Charlie's fingers danced over the control console, shutting down the ship's engines and opening the hatch. The older man turned to Rick and pursed his lips.

"This was my idea; I'll go first." Rick pushed from his chair and stood.

Drawing a steadying breath, he wedged his way through the resistance fighters and stepped outside, energy weapon cradled in his arms. To the right the door to Jace's skyfighter opened. He saw Mark's massive, shock trooper–disguised form exit the craft with a line of mock prisoners following him.

"Okay, move the animals out," Rick called back to Charlie as he lowered the smoky visor to his helmet. He lifted the rifle, finger curling around the trigger and resting there.

Taking his place beside Brad when the resistance leader shuffled from the craft, Rick walked toward the four shock troopers who stood guard at the processing center's gate. One of their heads turned. The shock trooper stared at the approaching procession, then nudged his companions. Rick tensed, ready for the whole insane charade to come tumbling down around his ears.

"Hey, you," a guard shouted. "Hurry up there. We've orders to move your prisoners directly into the processing queue. Commander Garth wants those skyfighters back into the air as soon as possible."

Thankful for the dark faceplate, which hid the relief that washed over his face, Rick released a soft sigh. He then grasped Brad's arm and shoved the man forward to hasten the pace.

"Back in the air?" the California resistance fighter questioned when two of the guards escorted him and the prisoners through the mass of people packed inside the fence. "We were supposed to be off duty two hours ago."

"Consider yourself lucky to be in the air," one of the shock troopers answered. "Garth has ordered double shifts here until the engineering teams can rebuild the processing centers the resistance has destroyed. Our only hope for relief is that the commander will return to the Mother Ship in Houston—soon!"

Rick pieced together the bits of information revealed in the soldier's few sentences. Apparently the Dallas–

Fort Worth resistance had made things so hot that this Garth, the commander of the Houston Mother Ship, had come to personally supervise the troops here. Rick smiled beneath the shield of his dark visor. The Forth Worth resistance would find an added prize waiting for them when they arrived.

"Commander Garth, the guards at the gate reported that the two skyfighters have landed," the sergeant at the communications console turned and called out. "The prisoners are presently being brought to the processing line."

"Good, good, Sergeant." Garth pushed from his chair and glanced at Major Lawrence. "Shall we go and see if the one I seek is among the prisoners?"

"Commander, photographs of the female were distributed to my pilots as you commanded. If this Sheryl Lee Darcy was among the humans, you would have been informed immediately," Lawrence answered.

Garth gritted a double row of reptilian teeth to hold back the curses that rode on his forked tongue. The major was incompetent and would be dealt with when time permitted. Now there were other matters with which to deal.

Without uttering a word, Garth strode from the communications room. Major Lawrence grunted, but followed. Down a dimly lit corridor and through a pair of sliding doors, the two Visitor officers moved, eventually reaching the heart of the processing center. Through this Garth also briskly passed, walking out the doors through which the line of humans entered.

"They should be at the end of the line." Major Lawrence pointed ahead. "There, I see one of the guards from the gate."

Brad nudged Rick's side. The resistance leader rolled his eyes forward. Rick's pulse raced at double time when

his gaze lifted. Fifty feet ahead of them in the line stood
Sheryl Lee. Her head was downcast, strands of her red
hair nearly covering her face, but there was no way Rick
could mistake the khaki-clad angel.

The young woman's face jerked up when a shock
trooper shoved her forward as the line shuffled closer to
the doors to the center. Rick tensed. A nasty purple bump
marred the smoothness of her brow. She *had* been injured
in the car wreck, or Visitors had inflicted the injury after
she had been captured.

Rick tried to tell himself the bruised lump didn't
matter; Sheryl Lee was alive! Now all he had to do was
gradually maneuver up the line so that he stood beside
her when the Fort Worth resistance force struck.

His gaze dipped to the watch on his wrist—four forty-
five. Fifteen more minutes. His temples pounded; at the
line's present rate, they would be inside the processing
center before the attack came. He had to come up
with . . .

"Lieutenant, are these the Dallas prisoners?"

A voice to the left fragmented Rick's thoughts. He
jerked rigid, his head snapping around.

"Commander Garth wishes to know if these are the
prisoners brought in from Dallas on the skyfighters." A
Visitor officer tilted his head to a man in a white uniform
beside him.

"Yes, sir." Rick forced himself to speak though the
cotton that suddenly filled his mouth.

"Where were they taken prisoner?" This from the
man in white—Garth.

The young man's mind raced. "East side, near the
Trinity River." The river was the only thing he could
immediately remember about the unfamiliar city.

Garth stepped along the line of twenty prisoners, then
shook his head. "It seems you were correct, Major
Lawrence. She's not here."

The two Visitor officers pivoted and walked back

toward the wide doors to the processing center. Again Rick gave silent thanks for the dark faceplate that hid his relieved expression. He glanced at his watch again. Five more minutes had passed.

"Major!" Garth's voice came from ahead.

Rick looked up; his blood ran cold. The commander of the Houston Mother Ship stood beside Sheryl Lee!

"I was right after all, Major Lawrence!" Garth took the young woman's arm and jerked her from the line. "Here is the female! You fool, she was only feet away from processing!"

Rick's temples pounded. This Garth wanted Sheryl Lee! *Why?*

"Who brought this woman in?" Major Lawrence's head jerked from side to side.

"My patrol, Major." A shock trooper stepped forward. "She was taken in a car chase with a ground patrol on the far south side of Dallas two hours ago."

"A ground patrol!" Lawrence repeated, his chest swelling defensively when he turned to Garth. "An honest oversight, Commander. Photographs of the female were distributed only to pilots—as to *your* orders."

Photographs . . . orders? Rick strained to hear every word, his confusion mounting by the second.

"Major, your pettiness is unbecoming an officer," Garth snapped. He would relish watching Lawrence slosh through the muck in the Mother Ship's septic tanks. "My task here is complete. Have a squad vehicle prepared for my return to Houston."

"Houston." The single word hissed between Rick's teeth.

"You heard the lizard." Brad wrenched a hidden energy pistol from inside his shirt. "We've run out of time! Now let's move!"

Raising the Visitor rifle to his shoulder, Rick sighted down the blue-black metallic barrel, taking aim at the center of Garth's back as the Houston Mother Ship commander led Sheryl Lee toward the processing center. Behind him the prisoner-disguised resistance fighters came alive.

"Commander!" Major Lawrence tugged at his holstered pistol while throwing out an arm and shoving Garth to the right.

Rick squeezed the rifle's trigger. Blinding energy burst from the muzzle in a crackling ball of fury that slammed into Lawrence's chest. The Visitor screamed as the deadly force of the impact flung him into two shock troopers behind him. All three fell, never to rise again.

"Move it, Rick!" Charlie pushed his friend forward. "He's got Sheryl Lee!"

The harsh barking of pistols and shotguns filled Rick's ears. He squeezed the energy rifle's trigger again, unleashing a string of bolts at four guards who rushed up the line toward his position, then he ran to the center's open doors.

Two more shock troopers pushed through the line of people. He fired again, hitting the closest with a blast that engulfed the alien's head. Charlie's beam sliced into the second soldier's chest. The black personal armor was of no avail; the Visitor crumpled to the ground.

"Get their weapons!" Brad shouted from somewhere behind the young Californian.

Leaping over the fallen shock troopers, Charlie and Rick darted into the processing center. In a quick glance Rick's gaze took in the ten stainless-steel-capsule stations that stood in a line at the center of the immense room he had entered. The heads of white-smock-clad Visitor processing attendants snapped around, their faces masked by confusion and fear. But nowhere did he see Sheryl Lee or Garth!

"Down!"

Charlie threw himself into the younger man. Together

they hit the floor rolling. Sizzling balls of energy splattered and flamed out on the walls behind them.

"The doors!" Brad shouted. "Close the doors. We can make a stand in—"

The resistance leader's command ended in a cry of agony! Two blue-white bolts leaped from out of nowhere and tore into Brad's back. With flames licking at his clothing, he toppled to the floor and died.

"There!" Charlie jabbed a finger toward the source of the bolts.

Shock troopers stormed through a pair of sliding doors to the left side of the processing room. Their black rifles blasted fiery death as they came. In a single heartbeat, chaos reigned within the immense center.

Chapter 22

Garth threw the red-haired human female behind a stack of empty capsules, drew his pistol, turned, and fired three quick bursts at the two humans in shock trooper uniforms who raced through the processing center's door. A curse hissed from his lips as the two leaped aside. He aimed the pistol again.

The ugly spitting of a machine gun came from directly ahead of him. He forgot the two and ducked behind the plastic containers. Whining slugs of angry lead ricocheted off the wall behind him—bullets meant for his chest.

Temples pounding, Garth suddenly comprehended the gravity of his situation. This attack meant more than the loss of another processing center; it could mean his own life—the life of a Mother Ship commander!

Sheryl Lee groaned to his left, her emerald eyes lifting. This female was what he had come for, and he had her. There was no need for him to remain here and die.

His head rose to poke above the stack of empty capsules. Shock troopers rallying to defend the center pushed into the main processing room from the center's interior. There was no escape through the sliding doors they came through or the center's entrance, which the resistance closed and blocked behind them.

Trapped! His mind raced, panic fed by five shock troopers who fell beneath a hail of bullets. His eyes dipped to the redhead for an instant. *It can't end like this! Not when I've gone through so much to get this female.*

Like a frightened animal, he darted a glance about the processing room. Hope vanquished the frigid sensation that clenched around his stomach like an icy fist. There was another avenue out of the room! The conveyer belt still moved, and it fed directly to the squad vehicles outside.

Stuffing the pistol back into its holster, he reached out with his good right hand, wrenched Sheryl Lee from the floor, and dragged her toward the conveyer belt.

Rick sprayed a barrage of bolts at the horde of shock troopers who attempted to press into the processing room. Five of the alien warriors toppled. In a scene reminiscent of the Visitors' trap at John Wayne International Airport, the fallen dead formed a bottleneck for those behind. Rick fired another blast and added a sixth red-uniformed soldier to those already piled on the floor.

"Rick!" Charlie nudged the younger man's shoulder as they lay prone on the floor. "Sheryl Lee!"

A glance in the direction of his friend's pointing finger revealed the Mother Ship commander across the room, tugging the redhead after him. "The bastard's trying for the conveyer belt!"

"Son of a bitch'll get to the squad vehicles outside!" Charlie squeezed off five sizzling bolts into the doorway.

His own safety forgotten, the young fighter ripped off his helmet and shoved to his knees. Firing a covering burst at the doorway, he bolted toward the processing units lined at the center of the room. Two bolts of blue-white energy tore at the floor ahead of him. He leaped the flames left in their wake and kept running.

Ahead he saw Garth throw Sheryl Lee atop the moving belt, then scuttle on after her. Then a field of spitting and hissing white fury rose in front of him!

Rick's brain barely registered the unexpected danger— one of the smock-clad Visitor attendants. His trigger finger simply squeezed without thought. Energy blasts sizzled and the acrid stench of burning alien flesh assailed his nostrils. The field of white fell at his feet, twitching spasmodically—death claiming another of the reptilian invaders.

"Sheryl Lee!" he shouted as the woman and the Visitor officer disappeared through a square-cut hole in the wall. "Sheryl Lee!"

Clambering over the barrier of alien equipment that separated him from the conveyer belt, he sprayed another covering barrage at the door, then jumped atop the belt. Two more Visitors in smocks raced after him. Swinging the energy rifle on them, he squeezed the trigger and left their bodies smoldering on the floor.

Rick dropped flat and came through the hole in the wall with his rifle ready for attack. The harsh glow of the perimeter floodlights gave him a clear shot at the back of the white uniform that raced to an open squad vehicle. He fired.

"Damn!" Rick watched the bolts crackle through the air, shoot over Garth's shoulder, and die in fiery blossoms inside the Visitor ship.

Searing heat flamed by Garth's face. He yowled in agony as the disguise covering his face melted. Releasing the redheaded female, he clawed at the makeup with his sole hand, to no avail. The human-imitating plastic welded itself to the vulnerable scaled flesh it hid.

Two more flaring balls of energy shot by his head. Enduring the burning pain that consumed the right side of his face, he reached out to retrieve Sheryl Lee. She was gone!

His head jerked from side to side. There to the right, he saw her stumble behind a squad vehicle. He took a stride after her and stopped. The ground before him exploded as energy beams ripped at the pavement.

The female could wait until another day. At the

moment he had to make sure that there would be another day!

He wrenched his pistol and hastily fired two rounds at the human who rolled from the conveyer belt, then he turned and darted inside the waiting squad vehicle.

Rick's shot splattered and flamed out on the closing doors of the alien ship as its engines whined to life. The craft lurched and wobbled, then shot up into the night sky. He fired two more bolts, which arced high to miss their mark.

"Sheryl Lee!" He turned his attention to his reason for being here. "Sheryl Lee!"

The redhead cautiously poked her head around the nose of a squad vehicle. "Rick, is that you? Rick!"

"None other!" He raced to her, scooping her into his arms and squeezing her tightly.

"Surfer Boy, I've never been so glad to see anyone in my life!" she managed to slur over a drug-thickened tongue. Then her lips pressed against his.

"Later, you two!" Charlie called out. "This ain't the time for snugglin'. We're right in the middle of a battle!"

Rick turned to see the older man come sliding out of the processing center on the conveyer belt. He opened his mouth to speak when the thunderous sounds of firing rifles tore through the night.

"The Fort Worth resistance!" He glanced at his watch. The attack was five minutes late, but they came.

Garth's half-exposed nostrils flared. The odor of burning plastic wafted in his nose. His gaze shot across the squad vehicle's control console—nothing!

A sputter of short-circuiting wiring came from behind him. Swiveling the pilot's seat around, he stared in horror. Flames and sparks leaped from the interior of the craft.

In an instant he realized that the blast that had melted his disguise had struck the inside of the ship, damaging the shuttle's circuitry. "Got to land," he mumbled aloud, cold fear creeping up his reptilian spine.

Turning the chair back to the control console, he reached out. . . .

Flames burst from the panel of blinking lights. The squad vehicle shuddered.

Garth's mouth opened. He sucked in one breath to scream a terrified denial of his fate. That "no" was never spoken. Flames flared, searing his lungs as he drew the last breath he was ever to know.

A nova rent the sky; daylight swallowed the night. A churning ball of red and orange flames erupted, dominating the heavens. Then, in the blinking of an eye, it winked out. Darkness crowded back across the heavens.

"Garth." Rick watched pieces of flaming debris stream downward like blazing meteors. "His squad vehicle exploded; why?"

Neither Sheryl Lee nor Charlie answered. They simply stood staring at the sky with mouths wide open.

Shouts, screams, the steady reports of barking rifles slowly penetrated Rick's dazed mind. His head turned to the processing center. "Fort Worth's resistance!"

"And we can give 'em a hand, son." Charlie nodded to the two skyfighters. "You up to a little aerial support for the ground troops?"

"Right!" Rick grinned and, with Sheryl Lee still clinging to him, followed the older man to the now abandoned gates of the center.

A line of shock troopers stood on the eastern side of the perimeter fence, their energy rifles spitting death at the small army that advanced across the floodlit terrain. The scene was far worse than Rick had imagined earlier. The resistance fighters were sitting ducks in the harsh glare of the lights.

"If you can let go of that pretty li'l' lady a moment or two, I could use a tailgunner," Charlie said as they entered the nearest fighter.

Rick reluctantly released Sheryl Lee and watched as Charlie helped her into the co-pilot's seat. The young man then took his place at the rear of the ship. He pressed the black button on the left side of the chair while Charlie brought the craft's engines to life. His thumbs rested on the firing buttons of the gun grips by the time the older man lifted the skyfighter into the air and swung it about.

"Go for the lights on the first pass," Charlie called out.

Which is exactly what Rick did. With the ship no more than twenty-five feet above the ground, he opened up with both barrels, his blasts picking off the lights Charlie missed with the nose cannons. Here and there he placed shots that rent wide, ragged holes in the chain-link fence surrounding the center.

The second run brought their full firepower to bear on the red-uniformed shock troopers defending the processing center. Like ants, the aliens scattered before the ground-ripping power of the craft's bolts. The aliens' flight was fruitless. At least half of the two hundred reptilian soldiers fell beneath the skyfighter's four guns.

The remaining Visitors died as the resistance assault force swarmed out of the night like a black wave.

Charlie hovered in the air until the last energy bolt flashed below, then he let the skyfighter drift to the ground. Ten minutes later five survivors of the Dallas resistance team packed themselves into the craft. The remaining five climbed into Jace's ship. Twelve of the twenty-four who had entered the processing center had been cut down, their bodies left where they had fallen.

Together the two skyfighters lifted into the air and banked eastward. From his tailgunner's seat, Rick watched the processing center recede, growing smaller by the moment. He barely blinked when the explosives set by the Fort Worth force went off. His mind was elsewhere, remembering a bear of a Texan named Mark who did not make the return flight.

Chapter 23

A piteous little moan broke the steady rhythm of Sheryl Lee's gentle breathing. The fingers of her right hand clutched at Rick's left. His eyes, more weary than sleepy, fluttered open.

Tense furrows ran across the redhead's brow, marring the peaceful mask of quiet sleep that had been there but moments before. She moaned again; her head tossed from side to side on the pillow.

"Shh," he whispered softly, and tightened his hand around hers. "Sleep and rest. It's all right now. Everything is all right."

Sheryl Lee's head jerked violently toward him. She whimpered like some small, frightened animal. Her eyes flew open, darting about a tiny room that contained only a chair and a small cot. Rick discerned the disoriented panic in her expression; it was as though she was uncertain where she was. Her fear-widened emerald eyes focused on his face.

"It's all right. You're back at Dallas headquarters." His voice came as a comforting whisper. He leaned forward and lightly kissed her forehead. "Go back to sleep and rest. You've been through a hell of a lot and need to sleep."

A smile of recognition lifted her mouth. Her right hand rose, fingers brushing over his cheek. "You need a shave, Surfer Boy."

He returned the smile and shrugged. "And you need to sleep."

"Have you been sittin' in that chair all night, lookin' after me like some mother hen?"

"Day. It's daytime, and it's only been a few hours," he answered, his eyes tracing over the delicate features of her face. In spite of the nasty purple bump on her head, she remained the beautiful fiery-haired angel who had greeted him aboard the *Wanda Sue* a lifetime or two ago. "You gave me a scare last night. I didn't think I'd ever see this beautiful face again."

"I told you once that line wouldn't work with me." Her smile widened while her fingers tightened about his hand. "I gave *myself* a pretty big scare last night. I remember the wreck and being thrown from it. That's when I hit my head."

She lifted her left hand to her forehead and winced when her fingers tested the nasty lump. "There were shock troopers comin' after us. I ran—thought I was runnin' from them. I didn't know where I was until I slammed head-on into three snakes."

Her eyes abruptly narrowed, and she stared directly into Rick's eyes. "Whose stupid idea was it to come after me?"

Rick masked his face with the most innocent expression he could contrive. "We can talk about that later. You need to rest now."

"It was your idea, wasn't it?" she pressed.

"I might have had a small part in it," he admitted. "I discovered that I'd grown used to having you around these last few days."

"It was stupid. You know that, don't you? Everything we've been workin' for here could have been destroyed last night. All of you might have been killed," she reprimanded him, but her hand remained about his.

"'Mights' don't count. Besides, who said we came after you? The last processing center in this area was destroyed last night. That might have been our real purpose for being there. Ever think of that?"

"*Might* have been, but it wasn't. You came there for me." Her emerald gaze caressed his features. "Stupid, Surfer Boy. But I'm damned glad you're on my side."

"Me too. Now try and get some more sleep." He leaned forward and kissed her brow again. "I'll be right here."

"I came within an inch of being killed in a car wreck last night, then the Visitors tried to make a frozen dinner out of me, and all I'm goin' to get is a peck on the forehead?" She frowned up at him. "They sure grow 'em shy in California."

"I . . . uh . . ."

Her left arm shot around his neck and eased his lips to hers. There was nothing shy or reserved in the passion of that kiss, nor in his own response. They clung together, arms wrapped about one another, hugging tightly, then in the next heartbeat their hands moved, stroking, soothing, speaking the desire of a man and woman.

He came to her gently, never questioning the swelling love that warmly opened within him, weaving out to melt and join with the love that radiated from the angel who gave herself to him. In a slow, rocking lullaby their bodies whispered all the tenderness the times and the circumstances had stolen from their voices.

When at last they lay quietly entwined on the small cot, he held her, and she cried, ridding herself, at least for the moment, of the demons of anguish and sorrow that she had locked within her breast for far too long. When the final shuddery sob passed from her body, he drew her even closer. Together they slept, protectively enclosed in each other's arms.

"We hurt 'em bad last night." Charlie sipped straight bourbon from a paper cup. "Gave 'em a thing or two to think about."

Rick poured a second shot in Sheryl Lee's own cup. She turned and smiled. Warmth suffused the Californian, and his heart quickened. The light of love that sparkled in those emerald eyes was meant just for him.

"Mind sharing that bottle?" Jace asked.

Rick passed the pilot the bourbon the four shared in memory of Brad and Mark and the others who had died in last night's attack on the processing center. A half hour ago the four had gathered in Brad's office to drink a toast in honor of their friends, a silent, personal wake of remembrance. But the weight of the world in which they struggled to survive had rapidly displaced the mourning, turning their thoughts and discussion to the Visitors.

"I'm not sayin' we didn't hurt 'em." Jace recapped the bourbon after pouring himself a second shot. "But it wasn't enough to stop the snakes."

"But you heard the message on the skyfighter's radio this mornin'." Charlie pushed back his gimme cap and glanced at his fellow pilot. "That Yvonne was appointed by Diana to replace Garth, and she's recalling the lizard troops in this area to the Houston Mother Ship."

"That will be for a few days, maybe a week at the most." Jace tossed down his bourbon, then crumpled the paper cup in his hand. "They'll try again, have no doubts about that. They'll keep tryin' again and again until they rob us of our world or we drive them back across the stars."

"Jace is right." This from Sheryl Lee. "The Visitors have lost their processing centers here, but they can—and will—build more. Until winter comes to give the red dust a chance to regenerate, Dallas and Fort Worth are open territory for the snakes. What we have to do is take advantage of the Visitors' temporary withdrawal and evacuate as many people as we can to the north."

"Which won't be enough." Jace's face twisted in disgust. "Soon as the lizards return, we'll be back in the same situation we've been in. Unless . . ." His voice trailed off and he glanced at the floor.

"Unless what?" Rick looked at the pilot.

"Jace and I were talkin' this mornin' while we were monitorin' the Visitors' broadcasts," Charlie spoke up. "We think that the run we made with the medical supplies shows that a pipeline for supplies and weapons can be established with the West Coast, and perhaps some of the northern states."

"Charlie thought he could use my Piper Cub to get him back to his own plane," Jace added. "From there he could fly on to Los Angeles. The Mustang is fast, and it's armed."

Charlie's head turned to Rick. "You're our only direct contact with L.A., Rick. Are you willin' to make one more flight with me?"

"Sounds like a ticket home to me." A wide grin spread across the young man's face. "But what about Sheryl Lee? Is there enough room for three people in the cockpit of a P-51?"

Charlie's gaze shifted to the redhead, and he chewed nervously at his lower lip.

Jace started to say, "Sheryl Lee isn't part of our . . ."

Sheryl Lee waved the man to silence. "I think Rick and I need to be alone for a minute. If you two wouldn't mind excusing us."

Rick's heart lodged in his throat as he stared into the green eyes that lifted to his. Charlie and Jace quietly rose and walked from the office, closing the door behind them.

"Jace was trying to say you weren't part of the plan, wasn't he?" he asked.

Sheryl Lee nodded, her eyes fixed to his.

"Well, you're part of my plans, dammit!" Rick said firmly. "I lost you once last night, and I don't intend to let that happen again for the rest of my life."

"I know." Sheryl Lee leaned toward him in her chair and took his hands. "It's a nice dream, isn't it, Surfer Boy? You and me livin', lovin', and growin' old together. I've got the same dream, and it means as much to me as it does to you. But we both know that it's only a dream—at least for right now."

"Dream? Don't tell me what we shared this morning was only a dream!" Rick's head moved from side to side in denial of her words. "I've never felt anything more real—neither have you."

"It was real, and that's what makes everything so damned hard. I love you, Surfer Boy. Love you more than is probably good for either you or me, because it's something neither of us can afford. It's a luxury we can't allow ourselves. There's a war goin' on, in case you haven't noticed. And you have to return to Los Angeles and—"

"You can come with me. We make a hell of a team, Sheryl Lee," Rick said, forcing himself to speak through the sudden dryness that filled his mouth. "We can—"

"Shh." Sheryl Lee pressed a finger to his lips. "I can't leave here any more than I can ask you to stay. This is my home, Rick. Los Angeles is yours. That's where you belong, where you can do your best in our fight against the Visitors. I can do my best here. I can't abandon what my mother and I have fought for this whole time."

Rick struggled to find an error in her argument and couldn't.

"One of these days the circumstances will be different. We'll be free to choose what life we want to live. Then—and I *know* that then will come—there will be time for two people. But not now."

"No time for two people, not with the whole damned world intruding." Bitterness swept through Rick. She was right, but he didn't have to like it.

"There is a little time—if we're willing to grab it and savor it," Sheryl Lee replied. "There's no possible way

Charlie will risk flyin' out durin' the day. It's only a few hours, and it's only a small room with a cot barely big enough for one person, but it can be ours. We can have what remains of this day."

Rick stood and reached down, drawing Sheryl Lee to him. His mouth covered hers. A few hours wasn't the lifetime of his dreams, but for now it was all they had, and he intended to do as she suggested—grab it and savor it.

The Piper Cub raced down the night-darkened street. Charlie Scoggin eased the controls toward him, and the single-engine plane leaped into the air, shooting over the roofs of the warehouses. The small craft banked to the left, heading toward Fort Worth to the west.

"We'll make my place in a couple of hours and with luck be in Los Angeles before daybreak," the older man said.

Rick didn't reply. Through tear-misted eyes, he stared downward, his neck craning to see the shadowy figure who stood below waving at the departing plane—a young redheaded woman who grew smaller with each passing second. His lips silently mouthed, "Good-bye, my angel. I'll be back."

And he would be too. Sheryl Lee had been right. One day there would be no Visitors to plague the world. How the reptilian invaders would be defeated and driven back to their own planet, he didn't know, but *they would be!*

On that day there would be time for two people named Sheryl Lee Darcy and Rick Hurley.

Watch for

PATH TO CONQUEST

next in the V series
from Pinnacle Books

coming in November!